ARROGANT PLAYER

JULIE CAPULET

Luna LaRoux has poured her heart and soul into her waterfront bar and restaurant, which has the best sunsets in Key West. The only problem is, Luna's best friend and business partner Josie is having money problems, and with twins on the way, Josie has no choice but to sell her half of the business. Actually, it's 51%.

Gage McCabe is spending the weekend in Key West when he happens to overhear an interesting conversation. Between a very pregnant majority shareholder and her stunningly beautiful—and deliciously desperate—business partner.

Gage can't resist. The bar is obviously a thriving business, and his new partner will just have to get used to *him* calling the shots…if she doesn't kill him first. It's this detail that frustrates him the most: she seems entirely immune to his charms. Unheard of. Gage is so sure of his own allure, he bets Luna his share that she'll surrender to him within a month—or the bar is hers.

Perfect. All Luna has to do is resist his drop-dead gorgeous looks, his smug charisma and his impressive… endowments, then she'll be rid of him for good. Easy, right?

1

PLINK. I drop one of the nails I'm holding and it splashes into the turquoise water below. I lean further over the railing of the deck of my Key West seaside bar—so far, in fact, that at any minute I might lose my balance and tumble headfirst into the water. I cling to the rough wood and feel a giant splinter slide deep into the pad of my thumb. "Shit." I ignore the pain as I hold the nail in place and bang it with my hammer.

"Now *that's* a view I could get used to."

I glance behind me.

It's Kyle, our busboy. He's a competitive weightlifter. He has veiny, pumped-up muscles that look manufactured and steroid-enhanced. "When are you going to go out with me, Luna?"

"I don't date employees, I've already told you that." Around seven hundred times. It wouldn't be appropriate.

Besides, he's not my type. Sure, muscles are great but not to the point of resembling an oily, spray-tanned Incredible Hulk.

"Need help?" he says.

"If it's the kind of help that means you get on with your job, then yes, that would be fabulous." I smile at him to take the edge off.

"Come on. How about one little after-work drink tonight?"

When hell freezes over, is what I'm thinking. I don't date pumped-up gym junkies. Or prowling suits on their conference business trips. Or drunk, over-eager tourists. And *definitely* not home-town jocks. I'm…between types at the moment. For reasons I don't dwell on, especially on a beautiful day like this one.

The sunlight glints off the water in shimmery flecks, glazing everything with its magic, or at least that's how it so often feels to me here in Key West. This little island has become my haven, as though the surrounding barrier of blue water is providing a necessary forcefield. Out there, beyond the Seven Mile Bridge, somewhere among the amber waves of grain and just before you get to the purple mountain majesties, lies my past and all my regrets. Here, I can breathe. The sugar sand and lush humidity comfort me in ways I didn't even know it was possible to be comforted. "See you inside, Kyle," I say lightly, pretending to threaten him with my hammer.

"Aw." He wanders off and I resume my work, leaning

a little further over the railing, holding on for dear life and desperately hoping I don't catapult myself overboard. I bang another nail into place.

"As if that's going to help," I hear another voice behind me say. I recognize the voice instantly as my best friend, the one and only Josie Farrell. My family moved into the house next to Josie's in Cedar Rapids, Iowa when we were both nine years old. I'd just arrived from New York City still in my city clothes. Josie saw me sitting on my front step, completely lost, like I'd spent so much of my childhood. Over the course of an idyllic summer, she showed me how to hand-squeeze lemonade. How to whistle with a blade of grass. How to find the best hiding places in the barn loft during our long hazy afternoons of playing hide and seek with her older brothers. How to get good height on the rope swing before you let yourself go, to get to the deepest, coolest water of the swimming hole. We've been inseparable ever since.

Her family became my family. My family is what you'd call…what's the word for it? Broken. Dysfunctional. Blended. Or some unhappy combination of all three. My parents divorced very un-amicably (i.e. they basically loathe each other) when I was six years old. My father ran off with his knocked-up (by him) secretary, who definitely didn't want a step-daughter in tow, especially one who was the spawn of her new husband's evil ex-wife. My mother is what you might generously refer to as a social climber. I think somewhere deep down inside her gold-digging heart she genuinely loved my father. The fact that their marriage imploded made her, in a way, give up on love altogether. So she went for money instead. Luckily for her, she was—and still is—beautiful enough to get away with it. Before the ink on her divorce papers was even dry, she moved us out of the only home I'd ever known and in with husband number two, a Manhattan real estate developer. I somehow found myself mired in the world of the super-rich. A limo driver drove me to my private school each morning. We had chefs and house-keepers, an indoor pool and gym, even a helicopter pad on the roof. My mother thought she'd died and gone to heaven. Me, not so much.

I discovered I'm not cut out to be super-rich. Maybe that sounds strange since so many people seem to crave it or aspire to it, but I just don't happen to be one of them. I spent three years living someone else's warped fantasy, which to me felt more like a gilded prison. Like being forced to wear a diamond-studded suit that didn't fit.

I prefer the simple things in life. A good friend to laugh with. A late-summer field of wheat to walk through. A beach at sunset. A cold beer after a hard day's work. People sometimes call me a hippie or a free spirit. I'm not sure if I'm either of those things. I am what I am, and it's…unique, so I'm told.

In Iowa, with its rolling hills and big blue skies, I finally felt free. I could get dirty and ride a bike and play flashlight tag in the dark. I could see the stars.

And Josie was there for all of it. Her family was every-thing mine wasn't. Big and loud and fun and close-knit. I found out what it feels like to laugh and to feel loved. It didn't matter that it wasn't my own family loving me. Josie's family felt more like mine than my own family ever has. So when my mother's second marriage fizzled out a few years later and she decided to move to Los Angeles for husband number three, I stayed with Josie.

The next two years ended up being a time of my life when I could have used a mother, as it turned out.

No one ever tells you the hard stuff can be harder than you ever imagined. No one tells you that some of that hard stuff is going to cut you down until you know for a fact you'll never be quite the same. Or that you're going to need more courage than you ever knew you had.

Somehow, I survived those two years.

The day after we graduated from high school, we jumped into Josie's beat-up old van and headed for Flor-ida. We couldn't get out of there fast enough. For her, it was her one chance to get out of the town she'd been born in and had never left. For me, it was a form of recovery. I needed to get out of that town like a drowning man in shark-infested waters needs a lifeboat.

We decided on Key West for no other reason except that we liked the sound of it.

And after three days of travel, as we drove through the tiny, sun-charmed, character-laden town, I knew I'd found the place I wanted to stay. Forever is a long time, but for me, something about the lazy heat that oozes out of this place answered a craving in my soul that was hard to explain. I still can't see myself ever leaving.

We got jobs as waitresses. We found a run-down one-room apartment, swam in the ocean and saved all our money. Turns out waitresses can earn good tips in Key West.

Three years later, when Josie's father died and left her a small inheritance (her mother had died years earlier, before I met her), we pooled all the savings we had, I sold an emerald bracelet Stepfather Number One had given me for my eighth birthday, and we somehow managed to scrape together enough money to put a down payment on a business that had just come up for sale. Our bar, where we'd worked all along.

It's a business that could do with a few upgrades. Okay, more than a few. It costs a lot of money to run—more than we ever anticipated, and exactly as much as it earns, barely—but I like a challenge. We jumped in at the deep end and we're trying like hell to learn how to swim. That was exactly ten months ago. "We're going to have to get this deck repaired by someone who actually knows what they're doing, Luna."

"I know. We will. But we can't afford to right now," I say cheerfully. I climb back over the railing. I'm wearing a cut-off pair of jean shorts and a fitted pink t-shirt with our bar's logo on the front. *Sea Breeze.* Which is now very dirty from my handywoman failure. The railing doesn't look any sturdier than it did five minutes ago. "Maybe a coat of paint will help."

Josie gives me a look. "Paint doesn't hold things together, Loon." It's the nickname she gave me a long time ago.

Josie has brown hair that's pulled back into a messy bun. Her dark eyes glint with that familiar twinkle and a slightly-exasperated expression. Her cheeks are pink with health and the kind of glow that could only mean one thing. Josie found out around six months ago that she got pregnant after a one night stand with a guy she never heard from again. The discovery was a shock, of course, and the past few months haven't been easy for her, to put it mildly. We cried together, because the whole scenario reminded us too much of the reason we left Iowa in the first place.

But once Josie got used to the idea, we decided there was no reason the two of us couldn't raise that baby right here in Key West. I promised I'd help her every step of the way. Of course I will. Besides, it won't be a bad thing for that little baby to grow up watching sunsets and playing in the sand, we figured.

"How'd your appointment go?" I ask her.

Her eyes fill with tears.

"Josie." Fearing the worst, I pull her into a hug. "What's wrong?"

"It's *twins*, Luna."

"Twins?" I pull back and hold her shoulders gently as I take in this information.

"Twin boys."

"Wow. Josie. That's …"

"Scary as fuck. I know. I don't know how to raise a baby by myself, let alone *two*. Luna, what am I going to do?"

I hug her again as she breaks down. She's done a lot of worrying over the past few months and I don't blame her. We have a budget health insurance plan that won't cover all her costs. Our bar gets plenty of customers but the rougher edges of the much-needed maintenance are really starting to show. Who am I kidding, they were always showing. It would be very easy to take this business to the next level—*if* we had a pile of cash to throw at it, which we don't. We tried to borrow more but the bank said we don't have enough equity. In fact the loan officer we spoke to was amazed we got the loan we did in the first place.

But we'll figure it out, like we always do. That's the thing about life, you *have* to figure it out. There's no other choice. "You're going to have those babies right here and we're going to take care of them together. On the beach, like we always talked about."

"That fantasy included true love and filthy rich men, Luna. Not destitute single mothers."

I don't remember the men being filthy rich in our fantasies, not mine at least, but I don't bother saying this.

As for the destitute single mothers comment, I let that slide. When you're seventeen and on the road to Key West, running from your past and finally excited about what your life might become, your fantasies star hot hunks with surfboards and a sensitive side. When you're twenty-three, alone, pregnant with twins and working all hours of the day and night to keep your struggling business afloat, I guess things tend to change. Anyway, I try to look on the bright side. "Everything will work out, Josie. You'll see."

"Would you get *real* here, please, Luna? I'm knocked up with twins by a man whose last name I don't even know who's now long gone. And I spent my inheritance on a failing business that needs a complete overhaul." I guess the pregnancy hormones are really starting to kick in. Then again, when she puts it like that, it does sound sort of dire. "Did you happen to see the latest online review, Loon? It went something like this: 'The food was hearty and the cocktails were strong as hell—and thank God for that because I needed four so I could concentrate less on my concerns that the dilapidated deck was about to collapse and hurl me into the sea, which, four cocktails in, would probably have drowned me.'"

I saw the review. Someone posted it last night. "That's our only one star review," I say defensively. It's the reason I got my hammer out this morning to see if I could try to spruce things up a little. But all I've got to show for my efforts is a big-ass splinter, blood dripping from my thumb and dirt all over my clothes. And what was I even thinking, trying to improve the look of the place with a hammer and a few nails?

But I'm a salt-of-the-earth type of girl. I don't sweat the small stuff. Not that being pregnant is small, but still. We've handled bumps in the road before. Including the bumpiest one of all, which I make a point of shoving back into its hidden corner of my most difficult memories.

"We'll figure it out, Josie. We'll get through this. Everything's going to be fine."

"*Fine?* How will it be fine, Luna? And how will we get through this? You don't *get through* parenthood. It's with you forever." The comment digs deep, for both of us. Tears pool in Josie's eyes. "I'm sorry, Loon. I shouldn't have said that." She hugs me. "Now I know how you felt," she sobs. I ignore her murmur. There are certain things from my past I definitely don't want to revisit right now. Or ever.

"Come on." I put my arm around her shoulders and lead her inside, where it's cool. One of our bartenders, Rico, just arrived and is starting to set up for the lunch crowd. I give him a little wave, grab some napkins and hand them to Josie. I help her up the back staircase that takes us up to our two-bedroom apartment. "It's not all bad. At least we *have* a business. An awesome one. It's what we always wanted. In time, it'll be just perfect."

I lead her over to the couch, which is in front of the windows and bathed in sunlight.

I love our apartment, even if it is "retro," as Josie generously describes it.

It's rustic and on the small side, but the views are to die for. From up here, when the sun sinks over the water, you feel like you're flying on wings made of gold. Like, despite the underbelly of desperation that sometimes infuses your days, from up here the melting horizon is so full of promise that nothing can touch you.

But now, in the blue light of mid-morning, things *have* touched us. Again. Very real things that are going to cry a lot and require healthcare and food and round-the-clock care and supervision.

"I'm going to call Owen," Josie says. Owen is her brother who lives down the street from their family home in Iowa, which is now owned by Josie's oldest brother Marlon. Her other brother Drew lives one street over. I can already see that it's this detail—one of the reasons we hit the road all those years ago in the first place—that's calling to her now. Five years ago, we couldn't imagine staying put like that. We were different from the people we knew. We had a wanderlust that no one understood except us. And I, in particular, had a lot to work through. I needed to leave, is what it boiled down to.

I bring her a glass of water and a box of tissues and set them down on the coffee table. "I'll go help get ready for the lunch crowd. You just relax and I'll bring you up some food."

"Thanks, Luna."

"We'll figure it out, okay?"

"Sure." She smiles at me weakly and it makes me sad that she's so beautiful and that the man who slept with her and left her in the dust with his babies on the way will never even *know*. We looked for him for months. He was blond and handsome and had a cool, surfie vibe—Josie's absolute weakness. *I didn't mean to have unprotected sex with him,* she sobbed after she peed on the stick and those two unmistakable blue lines showed up. *He told me he wasn't looking for anything serious. And neither was I! We just got carried away.*

It happens.

They will have made some beautiful babies.

But even though we wandered the streets and the hotels and the bars and asked around for a tall, sandy-blond Californian named Noah, he was already gone. The only thing our online searches revealed is that there are a lot of people named Noah in California.

And I don't like the defeated edge to her voice today.

I leave her to her phone call and walk past my tiny yoga studio where I do my practice every morning at sunrise. I go into my bathroom where I start stripping off my dirty clothes. I take a quick shower and pull on a sleeveless yellow sundress. I run a towel through my hair, which is dark and cut into an angled pixie bob. It has a wave to it that has a mind of its own. Even if I try to straighten it, within around five minutes it's starting to curl again, especially in the Florida heat, so I comb it into place and leave it at that. Then I head back downstairs to help Rico and the kitchen and waitstaff.

I don't care that our bar isn't the fanciest in town. It has *character*. It's funky and fun. Original and old school. It was a case of buying the worst business in the best location, because it was all we could (barely) afford. All the tables and chairs on the deck are colorful and festive, an effect that's enhanced by the shimmering blue water behind. We have a small beach and a dock where our customers can tie up their boats or park their jet skis. Our menu is basic American fare done well.

Maybe we could get another investor. Someone who has an interest in contributing money from afar, so Josie and I can continue to run our business without too much interference. We were only just getting going when Josie found out she was expecting. Her enthusiasm hasn't been quite the same ever since, with the morning sickness and the fear, but she'll come round again, once she has her babies and settles into a routine. We'll figure out how to grow the business *and* raise her little boys.

Everything will be fine.

2

GAGE

My phone rings in my pocket. I don't recognize the number but I answer it anyway. "Gage McCabe."

"Hi, Gage! It's Crystal."

Crystal. *Fuck. Which one was Crystal?* "Hi," I bluff, trying to make my voice sound at least mildly enthusiastic. "How are you?"

"I could be better …" Her voice lowers breathily. " … if you were doing that *thing* to me that you did in the back of your limo last weekend."

Ah. Now I remember. I picked her up at a fundraiser I went to last Saturday night. Blond. Fake tits. About as riveting to talk to as a doormat. I try not to focus *too* much on the flaws but there were a lot of them. As there always are.

I hadn't been interested at all until I was practically inebriated. Martini goggles changed my mind. "Yeah, that was fun." I run my fingers through my hair as I try to tone down my boredom. I need a haircut. Why the fuck did I give this girl my number? I think she might have insisted somewhere in the middle of round two of that *thing* I did to her in the back of the limo. The details are hazy at this point.

"God, Gage, you're so freaking *hot*. I want to see you again. Come visit me."

Fuck no. "I can't. I'm working."

She giggles, like she hasn't heard me correctly. "Just for the weekend. It would be *so* fun."

"No, I—"

"Guess where I am?"

I sigh. I'm not in the mood for this. "Where are you?"

"Poolside in my *very* skimpy bikini … in Key West!"

Yawn. "That's great. Well, hey, it was nice talking to you."

"Don't be so *boring*, Gage. Come visit. Live a little."

This almost makes me laugh. Give me a break. Live a little? Living a whole damn lot isn't my problem. I live in the fast lane and always have. The last thing I need is this silicone-enhanced bimbo telling me what I should or shouldn't be doing.

"It'll be fun," she coos.

I don't sleep with women beyond one night. It becomes tedious. They start thinking about commitment, it happens that fast. They latch on like barnacles if you let them get too close or start allowing them time. And commitment is very definitely something I don't want anything to fucking do with. "Listen, uh …" *What did she say her name was again?* "Crystal. I'm on my way to a meeting, so I'll——"

"Remember those cuff links you were wearing last Saturday? The ones with the rubies embedded into two linked circles?"

My father's cuff links. Given to him by my mother.

My fingers touch the cuff of my sleeve.

Fuck. I hadn't noticed they were missing. "You stole my cuff links?"

"I didn't *steal* them! I found them in my clutch. Remember one of them fell off when I tore off your shirt? I put them in there to keep them safe."

She stole my fucking cuff links. The only thing I own that has any real sentimental value. "I can't believe this."

"Gage, I did *not* steal them, you jerk! Come on. Come to Key West and get them. And have fun with me for the weekend while you do. It's a win-win."

A win-win. "Just have them couriered to me."

She giggles again. "Nope. You have to come get them."

"Look——"

"Gage, I'm lonely. And it's a long weekend. Don't tell me you've got meetings over Thanksgiving. That's a lame excuse. I've got a room with a view and I'm all alone. Pretty please?"

Goddamn it. I really don't want to lose those cuff

links. And now that I think about it, my cousin Travis emailed me a few days ago, saying he and his brothers are going to be in Key West this weekend. Their band is doing a tour and they have a private gig. They've been playing together since we were kids, but over the past two years they've skyrocketed to the big time. They've got the look. And their country-rock sound is distinctive. They sell out stadiums but every now and then they play smaller venues because they like the vibe, Travis said. He mentioned they've booked some off-the-beaten-track bar in Old Town and are closing it down for the night. When I got his email I didn't think much of it since I wasn't planning on being anywhere near Key West. But we've been talking about getting together for ages and this could be a good opportunity to catch up with them.

My phone pings with an incoming text. "I just sent you a photo," Crystal says. "Take a look."

Jesus. But I do it. I look. It's her, and she wasn't lying. Her bikini is skimpy as fuck. Showing off her fake tits in all their questionable glory. Which isn't doing anything for me. My martini goggles are long gone.

Another text comes through, with the name of the hotel and a room number. "So I'll see you tonight?" she asks.

"I don't appreciate being blackmailed, honey."

She laughs, as if this is some kind of fucking joke. "I'm not blackmailing you, Gage. I'm inviting you on a fun little getaway. Did you really have plans for this weekend?"

As a matter of fact, I don't. My brothers are both busy and so is everyone else I know. I can't stand the annoyingly ritualistic family get-togethers that go along with holidays, so I generally avoid them. I prefer spontaneity. That way, I don't have to be reminded of my own family's horrific tragedies, which always feel more raw around this time of year. My mother died the day after Thanksgiving and my father killed himself a few weeks later. But I'm not about to tell any of that to Crystal. "Yes."

She ignores this. "It's eighty-three degrees, the water's warm, the sun is shining and there's rum on tap. Take a break from frigid Chicago. I hear a cold front is moving in."

I glance out the expansive windows of my top-floor office. The sky is a dark, moody gray and the windows are flecked with icy rain.

Fuck it. I'll retrieve my cuff links then catch up with my cousins. "Fine. I'll see you tonight."

3

———

GAGE

THE SECOND MY private jet touches down on the tarmac in Florida, I realize this is exactly what I need. A break from Chicago, the shitty weather and the non-stop drama. Three women are currently threatening to kill me, two are stalking me because they think they're in love with me and one might actually have taken out a hit on me because all week I've had the feeling someone has been following me.

Whatever.

These things are a side effect of my lifestyle, which I don't plan on changing any time soon.

They accuse me of being an asshole, a player, a commitment-phobe, a prick.

I don't deny any of these charges.

At least they can't accuse me of being a liar. I am what I am and I'm straight-up with them from the get-go.

I tell them point blank I'm incapable of commitment. The mere thought of a long-term relationship practically gives me hives. Being with someone for more than a week makes me insanely restless and borderline insane, like a rabid caged animal. I tried it once.

This is possibly because I witnessed true love in its purest form in the relationship of my parents. They *adored* each other. To the point where it now seems like a once-in-a-lifetime kind of scenario. A star-crossed lucky score. They were careful and kind and thoughtful with each other. They laughed a lot. They had fun together. They respected each other's eccentricities lovingly, almost worshipfully. Like they loved each other's uniqueness far more than the normal details—my mother's tendency to disappear into her work studio for days on end to create her wild, whimsical clothing designs; my father's mad-scientist approach to investing his money and building houses and boats and gardens that were more than a little outrageous.

I've never seen a man so in love with his wife as my father was. But it only ended up destroying him. When my mother got sick, he went mad with despair. When she died, he just couldn't handle it at all. So he hung himself with a short rope from one of the beams in our garage.

Luckily for me, I'm incapable of love so I won't have to suffer the same fate. After seeing what it did to my father, I'm *glad* I'm incapable of it. Devastation on that level isn't something I want to experience. I loved her too, of course. And I was also devastated, like we all were. But for him it was different. He just couldn't fathom a life without her. He simply didn't want one.

I can't imagine adoring a woman or caring *that* much about anything at all.

I've never felt even an inkling of *adoration*. Lust, sure. Affection, maybe, once or twice. But the whole topic of true love bores me to tears. Unlike my father, I'm far more likely to find a woman's quirks crushingly annoying than cute and endearing. I can't laugh at inane jokes that aren't funny *just* because I'm into the person telling them —because I'm *not* that into them. Ever. Most of the time I don't even *like* them. Every single time, all I'm thinking about is how to end it.

For better or worse, I don't have it in me to love like that.

I've come to terms with my limitations. The word marriage gives me an allergic reaction and I've never felt any emotion even close to jealousy or possessiveness or a longing for more. I have no interest in anything more prolonged than a very temporary happy ending.

So I've accepted my fate as a bachelor and a player. I'm rich as fuck, I'm 6'3" and built like a porn star (their words, not mine, but I'm hardly going to argue). Because of my money, my status as an investment prodigy, my looks and my so-called style, I've achieved a certain amount of pop culture fame. I ranked fifth on People's Sexiest Man Alive list last year and soon after that I was photographed for the cover of GQ, which did a feature on me. After that it was the Wall Street Journal, then Forbes. "The savvy of Warren Buffett meets the allure of a young George Clooney," was the headline. Which made me laugh. I couldn't care less about shit like that aside from the obvious perk of having women dropping their panties at the snap of my fingers because of it.

But right now I'm seriously regretting the whole thing with Crystal. My plan at this point is to get my cuff links and get the fuck out of there. She can blackmail me into coming to Florida but there's no way in hell I'm spending the entire weekend with her.

I disembark from my jet. The flight attendant—a new one—smiles at me demurely. I wink at her and she blushes. Maybe on the way home I'll give her what she wants. I walk over to my waiting car, pulling out my phone as I give the driver the hotel address and slide into the back seat. As we start driving, I call Travis.

"Gage," he answers. "Good to hear from you, man."

"I just landed in Key West."

"No shit. Come to our show on Friday night. The venue's location has been changed twice because the info leaked and they don't want it getting swarmed. I'll text you the address on Friday and I'll let the door people know you're coming."

Friday is two days from now. "You in town tonight?" I ask hopefully.

"No, we've got a sold out show at Greensboro tonight.

We're still in North Carolina. We get to Florida at around noon on Friday."

Damn. "How's the family?"

"Good, man. Everybody's good. When are you and your brothers coming to Nashville? We need a family reunion one of these days."

"Yeah, we're overdue."

"I hear Caleb's home. How is he?"

My brother just got back from a year-long tour of duty in Afghanistan. He came to see me out of the blue a week or two ago and is suffering pretty intensely from the effects of PTSD. Even worse, he thinks he's in love with some girl he just met. "He's okay. He just needs a little time to adjust to normality again."

"I bet. What are you doing in Key West?"

Good question. "Just…uh, visiting a friend."

"Oh yeah? Bring her to the show on Friday."

"No." *Fuck no.* "It's nothing like that."

Travis laughs. "Cool. Talk to you soon, then. Happy Thanksgiving, bro."

"Yeah, you too. Give my best to everyone." There are four siblings in their family. They all live in Nashville and they're all involved in the Tucker Brothers Band. Travis is the lead singer, Vaughn is the drummer, Kade plays bass guitar and the youngest, Roxie, is their manager. It'll be good to catch up with them. It's been too long.

By the time I end the call we're driving through Old

Town, with its quaint storefronts and restaurants and its lively bars. It's busy tonight with the holiday crowd.

We turn the corner and pull up in front of one of the waterfront resorts. It's been a few years since I was in Key West but you never forget the smell, of sea salt mixed with faintly decaying sargassum. The thick humidity of the air feels good after the driving sleet of Chicago.

When I walk into the lobby of the hotel, where the sliding doors are open to the wraparound deck, Crystal is waiting for me. Sitting at a table in a small alcove by the window. She's sipping from a large glass of wine, scrolling on her phone. With a good view of the front door. She sees me immediately. Her face lights up and I'm not proud of myself for thinking it, but all that comes to mind is, *Wow, my martini goggles were working overtime that night.*

Don't be an asshole, Gage. She's not ugly. She's just…not someone I really want to spend more than the next three minutes with.

"Ga-a-a-ge!" Crystal squeals, teetering over to me on sky-high heels in a ridiculously tight dress. She's wearing full make-up and her hair has been sprayed into place with possibly an entire can of hairspray. "I'm so excited! We're going to have *such* a fun weekend!"

"Hey," I manage, my mind busy thinking up an easy excuse.

She kisses my cheek and I allow this, but I can't bring myself to return the favor. Her perfume wafts and I almost recoil, but catch myself. "Come have a drink with me," she says.

"Let's get the reason I'm here dealt with first, sweetheart." I'm not playing games with this chick.

She blinks at me as we sit on the tall stools on either side of the table, like she's mildly offended that's the first thing I would say. "That's not the *only* reason you're here," she coos.

Actually, honey, it is.

But she opens her purse and pulls out my cuff links, placing them on the table. I slide them into the pocket of my jacket.

"I didn't steal them." She smiles, taking a sip of her wine. "But it was a good excuse to see you again."

"No harm done." She's lucky I can use this as a reason to catch up with my cousins this weekend, or I'd be far less understanding.

The waitress appears. "Can I get you a drink, sir?" Her eyes rove my face, to my body and back to my face again. "Oh my God. You're Gage McCabe!"

It happens. People recognize me more and more these days.

"I read about you!" the waitress gushes. "After I read that article about you in the Wall Street Journal I got inspired enough to start my own portfolio. It's not much, but it's already gone up a little. God, I would *love* some advice if you ever have time. I mean, I'm sure you don't but—"

"He doesn't," Crystal scowls, staring icily at the waitress.

The waitress glares back, but then, mindful of keeping her job, possibly, she curbs her enthusiasm. "Of course you don't. Um, what can I get you then, Mr. McCabe?"

"Jack Daniels on ice."

The waitress glances at me longingly, then saunters off to the bar.

"Wow," Crystal laughs. Her eyes are a dull shade of brown that's hard to describe. The color of sargassum, maybe. "The wolves are already descending," she says. "Not that I'm surprised. You look amazing, like always."

I don't bother replying. I pull off my tie and loosen the collar of my shirt and she stares at me sort of hungrily as I do this.

"But you're all mine this weekend, Gage. You promised." Did I? Not quite. "You must be tired after your trip. Let's take our drinks back to the room."

I don't bother telling her that traveling in a private jet isn't tiring at all. Neither is getting driven around by chauffeurs. Any mention of private jets and limos to the women I date—if you could call it dating—is basically like waving a T-bone in front of a starving dog. They get even more clingy. The visions of two point five kids and summer houses by the lake (which I own several of) start flitting across their expressions.

She reaches to hold my hand but I slide it away before

she notices my dodge. Usually I'd take the easy lay, but something about the color of the sunlight on the water tonight changes my mind. It's so…beautiful. I have a brief and very unfamiliar urge *not* to engage in dirty deeds done dirt cheap, for once in my life. Maybe it's the holiday weekend that's messing with my head, but for a second I wonder what it would feel like to actually *want* to spend time with the person you're with, instead of only being interested in fucking just for the sake of it.

Hell.

Where did *that* train wreck of thought come from?

And where's my damn drink?

I'm relieved when Crystal's phone rings. "It's my boss. Gage, do you mind if I take this?"

"Go right ahead."

She gets up from the table and wanders out to the deck to take the call.

I look past her, to the dazzling colors of the sky. That sunset really is something. The vibrant hues are melting over the horizon, lighting up the expanse of mirror-calm water and painting everything with surreal shades of bronze and gold.

The waitress reappears, delivering my drink. Her smile is professional but the look in her eyes is hot and determined. It's not hard to decipher what she wants. The same thing they all want. She has mousy brown hair that's been dyed with tints of pink. She thinks of herself as a rebel, willing to cross lines, but her insecurities override these tendencies. In bed she'd be submissive and grateful.

She leans closer, her voice breathy. "I would *really* love to meet up with you later, Mr. McCabe. My shift ends in twenty minutes and my apartment isn't far from here. I'm *such* a huge fan. That article said you were single," she adds, glancing toward Crystal. "*And* that you're a playboy. Is that true?"

I don't bother confirming or denying. I know all about the effect I have on women and this one's no different. They're biologically hard-wired to throw themselves at the rich, hot, buff alpha male. Someone who's virile and loaded, who can provide for them and make all their dreams come true. Some glitch in the natural order of things means they see all that in me. They can't help themselves but to climb over each other to get close to me. Most days I revel in that shit. Tonight—fuck knows why—I'm not feeling it. I'm having some sort of weird, sunset-warped mood swing I can't explain.

I tip back my drink.

The waitress scribbles a phone number onto a cocktail napkin and slides it toward me.

Just then Crystal reappears. I grab the damn thing and jam it into my pocket, more to get rid of it than for any other reason.

Crystal glares at me. Then she glares at the waitress, who's standing just a little too close to me, gazing at me with that starving-dog eagerness.

"Is that her *phone number*?" Crystal seethes.

The waitress's eyes gleam at Crystal competitively. "I wanted to ask him for some investment advice, that's all."

Crystal picks up her glass of wine and throws the contents of it in my face.

"For fuck's sake," I mutter.

"How *could* you, you asshole!" Crystal shrieks at full volume, so that everyone in the bar turns to look. A woman in a cheap polyester suit strides over like she's on wheels. She's wearing a badge that says *Duty Manager.* "Are we having a problem here?" To Crystal. Like *she's* the one who's been wronged. But then the woman's gaze slides back to me. She's got to be pushing forty and that suit is doing her no favors. I see the second it happens, when her outrage is overridden by interest, which devolves quickly into lust. *Jesus.* I hate to sound ungrateful here but sometimes being irresistible to women is a goddamn curse.

I stand up and sling my bag over my shoulder. "No problem at all. I was just leaving. Happy Thanksgiving, ladies."

I throw a fifty dollar bill onto the table to pay for my drink and walk the fuck out.

4

GAGE

I USE the cocktail napkin to wipe most of Crystal's drink from my face, then toss it. Eventually my shirt will dry in the breeze. At least I can be glad it was white wine.

I take my time, strolling along the waterfront, with its bars and restaurants and rowdy crowds of tourists making the most of the long weekend. Couples are milling around, hand in hand, and I feel that strange pang again. What would that *feel* like? To want to spend an entire four-day weekend with the same person?

Who cares, my subconscious insists.

Most likely, I'll never know.

I'll do what I always do. I'll find a place to have a drink, I'll make eye contact with the most beautiful woman in the room, who will inevitably fall for me. I'll gauge whether it's worth it, if there's a boyfriend or husband and how livid the look in his eyes is. She'll give me signals. *Just say the word and I'll ditch him,* is usually where it leads. It's that easy. I'll take her back to a hotel—there's always a spare suite if you offer a high enough price, no matter how busy the night is—we'll fuck and it'll take the edge off of my restlessness and my ennui for an hour or two. She'll beg me to stay. I'll refuse, and life will go on as it has ever since I hit puberty.

Actually, my playboy mentality started well after that. It became a coping mechanism when the world tilted off its axis after my parents clocked out. I was already living in Chicago at that point, but life took on a more cynical, pessimistic edge. When a love story of my parents' caliber gets snuffed out in the most painful of ways, it recasts your outlook. A psychoanalyst might say I was attempting to fuck the grief out of my system, unsuccessfully.

I don't actually think it's that complicated. I do it because I feel like doing it. And I walk away for the very same reason.

The women I've known are right to accuse me of being heartless and cold. I am. I feel nothing when they cry, aside from irritation and a need for distance, once my physical urges have been met.

I'm a total prick, they tell me. And they're right. I buy and dismantle businesses people have spent a lifetime building. I use women. I wave money and the promise of hot sex around to get whatever I want, damn the consequences or the heartbreak along the way.

None of it tends to bother me. I give shitloads of my

money to charity, maybe in an attempt to level the score, who knows.

I can't apologize for who I am. More accurately, I *won't* apologize for who I am. Whatever made me this way, fate or circumstance, it doesn't really matter. Women love me regardless. They crave a one night stand they can brag about to their friends before they retreat into their mediocre relationships and unfulfilling sex lives. They follow me and stalk me and beg for more. They cry and fall in love and occasionally threaten to kill me. Because I make them feel like no one else can. I take them places no one else has. I'm what every woman wants but very few can actually get.

Tonight, for some reason, my lifestyle sits more heavily than usual. I'm twenty-seven years old. Do I really want to live the rest of my life as an asshole and a manwhore?

Of course I do. Why wouldn't I?

A rare wave of loneliness hits me somewhere in the middle of my chest.

I almost laugh. *Hell.* I'm a player, I remind myself. Not some brooding goddamn romantic, like my brothers have suddenly morphed into, to my intense disgust.

What I need is another drink. I'll drown whatever this passing wave of weakness is. I'll catch up on some sleep. I'll meet up with my cousins. Then I'll return to my who-gives-a-fuck lifestyle. Chicago's a good place for that. It's easy to disappear into my haven of wealth, where no one and nothing can touch me.

The warm weather down here in Key West seems to be thawing out something inside me. I'm not sure the feeling is a good one.

I get to the end of the row of restaurants, where a wide-open dock area is scattered with public benches and colorful flags that wave lightly in the tropical breeze. A jazz band is playing from a raised stage at one end. A crowd has gathered.

The red sun dips its lowest edge into the farthest point of the ocean, painting the sea, the sky and the world itself in various shades of crimson, almost like the night is on fire.

The last bar of the long row is small and quaint. The place could do with some refurbishments, but its large deck is inviting, with colorful tables and a killer view. I decide to grab a drink and some dinner.

I step inside.

The interior is infused with old-Florida charm. The walls are rustic, unpainted Dade pine and the bar is lit with hanging pendant lights. The many sets of French doors that lead out onto the expansive deck are open, so the red sunlight spills in and gives the whole place a warm, tinted glow.

It's busy but not overly crowded. I can't help thinking they could do a lot more with this place. It's an absolutely prime location. There's a jet ski dock and even a small sandy beach.

I walk up to the bar where a bartender is polishing glasses.

"What can I get you?" he asks.

"A Dos Equis with a lime wedge and a Jack Daniels on ice." Might as well get shitfaced after the day I've had. At least I got my cuff links back.

I take a seat at the far end of the bar, next to the open set of doors, that takes full advantage of the view. My drinks are served and I order a steak. Then I scroll through a few of my messages and my stats.

It's then that two women enter the bar through a side door behind me I hadn't noticed until now. One follows the other behind the bar. They must work here.

One of the women is roundly pregnant, with tied-up brown hair and pink cheeks. Her eyes are bloodshot and shiny, like she's been crying.

The other is slim with dark hair that has sun-bleached highlights that look almost shockingly natural. Most of the women I associate with couldn't do natural to save their lives. I can't see her face from this angle, but something about the way she moves holds my attention. She's wearing a yellow sundress with no sleeves. Her shoulders and arms are smooth-looking and lightly tanned. Her skin, I notice even from this small distance, is absolutely flawless. "Josie," she's pleading, "you *can't*. I won't let you. I know you'll regret it."

"I don't have a *choice*, Luna. Owen said he's doing up his barn into an office and a two-bedroom apartment. He said I can live in his main house for free. He's even going to hire me part-time to do his books. That means he can add me to his health insurance policy, which I desperately need, obviously. His plan is a lot more comprehensive than ours."

"But, Josie…it's in *Iowa*."

"So's my whole family." The pregnant woman sighs, like the weight of the world is on her shoulders. "I can't do this alone, Luna."

"You're not alone. You've got me."

The pregnant woman stares at her friend, and a tear traces a line down her cheek. "And I *love* you, sweetie, you know that. More than anyone. But I'm about to have *twins*. I'm terrified. I'll have half a dozen babysitters at the ready, a house, a work-from-home job and the use of Owen's car. He said he never even uses it and that he can write it off as a business expense. He got a new pick-up truck a few months ago."

"But—"

"I've already made up my mind, Loon. I'm going home."

"But *this* is your home now."

"It's more your home than mine," the one named Josie says. "It always was. I never intended to move here *forever*. We've had an amazing time, but it's not the right place for me anymore. I mean, I'll have to think about schools and backyards and carpools…the kind of things my brothers already have. My babies will have cousins and aunts and uncles and a *home*. I need to do this."

"But…what about the bar?" says the dark-haired girl. As she turns slightly, I can make out the contours of her profile. She has long, curved eyelashes, a perfect nose and lips a fraction too full. Her breasts are insanely pert and soft-looking, tapering down to a slim waist, flared hips and long, coltish legs. Despite all her femininity, there's something almost tom-boyish about her. There's a light sprinkling of freckles across her cheeks and the bridge of her nose. She has a quirky bob hairdo, flicking in impertinent little waves that curl against her graceful neck.

Jesus.

My heartbeat lurches into an up-tempo beat and my chest feels weirdly hot.

She's cute as fuck.

Luna, her friend called her.

Not my usual type at all, but seriously gorgeous, in a young, sassy, carefree kind of way.

Another tear draws a shiny line down Josie's face. She takes Luna's hand. "I'm going to have to sell my half. It's the only way I can afford the medical costs, the food, the equipment, the clothes and whatever else babies need. I'm going to need *money*, Loon. As much money as I can get my hands on. It's the only way I'll possibly survive this."

Luna's face looks stricken. This detail is strangely

unacceptable to me. Why, I have no idea. "Sell?" she says. "But…to who?"

"We'll find a silent investor," Josie says. "You know, someone who can contribute from their office in New York or somewhere. So you can make all the decisions and run the place without having to answer to anyone."

Luna smiles weakly. "I'm sure such a person exists."

"We'll never know unless we advertise. We might be surprised."

"But, Josie, are you sure you really want to do this?"

"I *don't* want to do it, Luna, not at all. But this isn't about me anymore." Josie places her palm on her stomach. "It's about them. These babies. I have to do what's best for them now."

I'm mildly impressed by Josie's dedication. Whoever the father is, he's clearly out of the picture. I'm also impressed by the way Luna shakes off her obvious fear over the impending situation. In fact, I'm inexplicably riveted by this entire conversation.

Luna gently squares her shoulders. "All right. Yes. You're right. If that's what you want to do, then I'll help you get your money out of the business. I just have one request before we try to find an investor."

"Anything."

"Let me buy out two more percent, so I have the majority share."

"Oh," says Josie. "I forgot about that. That's right, I

own fifty-one percent." She considers this for a few seconds. "Why did we do that again?"

"Because Marlon acted as a guarantor. It was the only way we could get a mortgage that big. We figured that was worth a few percent, remember?"

"Oh, yeah."

Luna glances at a customer, who's sitting down onto the bar stool next to mine. A woman. Blond. Full make-up. She might have stepped out of the same styling school as Crystal. Come to think of it, most of the women I've been with over the past year could have stepped out of the same styling school as Crystal. *Why do I always go for the vapid, trying-too-hard-but-never-quite-succeeding dye-job desperados?*

It's then that two things happen. I get my first real look at Luna's face as her glance falls lightly onto me. As I do, I can admit it's a moment that I know will stick in my mind for…I hate to say *eternity*, but there it is. She's fucking *stunning*. It's a pure, offhand beauty that hits me right in the beat of my own heart. And lower. I can feel myself getting hard right here at the bar.

Fucking hell.

But there's nothing I can do to stop the effect she's having on me. I want to take her somewhere. I want to stare at her for a while without interruption. You can tell she wakes up in the morning like this. Tousled and bright-eyed with fresh, dewy skin and those naturally bee-stung lips.

I want to wake up with her. After spending the night tasting every inch of that smooth skin and those petal-pink lips.

What the fuck?

I don't *wake up* with women. I leave when I'm done with them.

As she briefly contemplates me, I wait for the fascination to take hold. The usual awe. But if she notices me at all, it's light and fleeting. Her attention is already being diverted back to the conversation with her friend.

Wait, I want to say. *Don't turn away from me yet.*

I have a strong urge to interrupt her.

"Well, there's an easy solution to the fifty-one percent," Josie is saying. "I'll gift it to you. We'll write it into the contract that whoever buys my half is buying forty-nine percent."

"Okay. Yes." Luna pauses. "But let me give you something for it. I don't have any cash in the bank but—"

"No, Luna. It's a gift. I'm not going to leave you in the lurch. I'll make sure you're okay, you know that. I'm going to make sure you're happy with whatever the arrangement is."

What is it about this exchange that's hitting me right where I live?

I don't know.

I don't fucking know.

But as I watch this strangely beguiling girl in her yellow dress with her sun-kissed skin and her eyes which I can see in the golden light are green and flecked with color, like her pupils are emitting some glowy, mesmerizing light that I want to attract in ways I really don't fully know how to fucking analyze, something's happening to me.

Don't be a goddamn sap, you idiot. She's gorgeous, that's all. Something's not "happening to you." You want to take her to bed and feed on all that cute-hot beauty, that's what's "happening." You want to peel off that yellow dress and suck on her cherry-ripe nipples which you can just barely see the outlines of under the thin fabric. Then you want to do unspeakable things to that sweet, luscious mouth.

I look for the inevitable flaws, which are usually the first thing I notice. But what's fascinating me is that…*there aren't any.* Her face is outstandingly…symmetrical. Her eyes are bright and clear. And determined.

Luna from Iowa. Luna with the soulful eyes and angular shoulders and the vibrant allure that's more real than I know how to handle.

Goddamn it.

Maybe I've had more to drink than I realized.

"Hey," someone next to me says. My concentration diverts briefly to my left.

It's the blond. She's checking me out.

"What brings you to Key West on a Thanksgiving weekend?" She blinks her lashes at me, which are thick with caked mascara. I stare at her for a few seconds and there they all are: the flaws. The overdone makeup. The smile that does nothing to hide the desperation in her eyes. The hunger for things I can give that have nothing to do with the person I am.

Since when did that matter?

"Business or pleasure?" she says coyly.

My gaze slides away. I'm staring. Not at the blond, but at the girl in the yellow dress.

"Pleasure," I reply.

Hers.

And mine.

5

I CAN'T BELIEVE it's come to this. My bestie is bailing on me.

Of course I understand why. But Iowa, our past, our families—or what remains of the wreckage, in my case at least—feels a million miles away.

Can I do this alone?

I take a deep breath.

Of course I can.

I can.

We'll get an investor who will pump a huge cash injection into our—my—business and everything will be wonderful. Josie will go home to Iowa and be welcomed into the loving circle of her supportive family where her twins will be well taken care of. And so will she. It's all for the best.

And me?

I feel like more of an orphan than I ever did when my parents left me.

Suck it up, Luna. You're twenty-three years old. You're quirky and energetic and capable. You can do anything you set your mind to.

Can I?

Yes.

I'll figure it out.

I'll *have* to figure it out.

Josie's eyes are bloodshot and her eyelashes are wet and spiked like art deco designs. *Noah,* I can't help thinking, *you really missed out on something spectacular.* She looks so tired. I guess growing two babies inside your body is going to take its toll. And she hasn't even gotten close to the hard part yet.

"Right now," I tell her, "I want you to go upstairs and relax. Sleep for a while. I'll help Rico until the rush is over and then I'll come upstairs and we'll figure out exactly what we're going to do. Okay?"

Josie wipes her eyes, but they're still leaking. "Okay. I'm so sorry, Loon. I'm sorry about everything."

I give her a hug. "Don't say that. There's nothing to be sorry about. Everything happens for a reason. Those *twins* are the reason. Those little babies are going to light up your life in all the best ways. They'll have a fabulous life back in Iowa with their tree houses and their swimming holes and their carpools and their cousins."

I gently guide Josie back toward the door that leads up to our apartment and I send her on her way. She's so emotionally fragile these days, breaking down at the drop of a hat. Yesterday she cried her eyes out over a dog meme she saw on Instagram. She needs to rest.

Once she's gone, I turn my attention to the customers. The place has filled up and there are ten or so people seated at the bar.

A man is watching me. He's been watching me for a while. His drink is empty. I walk over to him. "What can I get you?" He's dark-haired and good-looking—like, *insanely* good-looking—in a smug, over the top kind of way. The kind of way that guarantees he could and probably has banged every woman in sight for most of his adult life. I can't tell if the woman sitting next to him is his date or not. If she is, he's giving her the cold shoulder and this annoys me.

"Can I buy you a drink?" he asks me. So she must not be his date.

Arrogant doesn't even scratch the surface with this one. This guy could probably give a master class on the subject. "Thank you, but no. I don't drink when I'm working." I glance at the blond woman, who's staring at the guy like he's the answer to all her prayers. "But *she* looks like she might want one," I suggest.

"All right, then," he says, without missing a beat. His voice is deep and has a smoky husk to it that's almost comically sexy. No doubt women fall at his feet. Luckily, I won't be one of them. I learned my lesson a long time ago. Guys like this one—the "alphas," who every woman in the room watches and covets and wishes was hers, are the ones who will destroy your life. I should know. It happened to me once and I honestly don't know if I could survive a second round. So I go out of my way to avoid smug jerks like this one, especially ones whose collar is barely dry from the wrath of the last woman he scorned. When you work in a bar you learn the signs. "Put her drink on my tab. I'll have another Jack Daniels on ice. And when your shift ends, I'll buy you whatever you want."

He's outrageously sure of himself. Most people I deal with on a daily basis have threads of insecurity to their overall manner, but this guy doesn't. And neither do I. My mother once told me she's never met anyone as brave as I am. Not that it's helped me all that much, but for some reason this guy reminds me of that quality in myself. Like I'll need all the bravery I can muster when he's around. Which is a weird thing to contemplate, but there it is.

"My shift never ends." I'm trying hard not to be rude to him, but my emotional scars are lighting up and my heartbeat is racing. I add three ice cubes to a glass and pour his whiskey.

He cocks his head slightly. His eyes are an unusual shade of aqua, rimmed by dark, dense lashes, quietly challenging me. There's a rough, masculine glamour that clings to him like he's been sprinkled with angel dust. He's extraordinary, one of nature's chosen ones.

I have to hand it to him, he's bringing his A game to the tomcat-on-the-prowl playbook. Unfortunately, I already know how the story ends.

With fear. With not being able to escape. With the realization that you've just made the most painful mistake of your life. With the kind of regret that digs in and won't let go.

Damn. It's been a while since my old damages have felt so close to the surface. I take a deep breath. *I'm good now,* I remind myself. *I'm over all that.*

"All work and no play is bad for the soul," he purrs. "Everyone's shift ends eventually."

After almost a year of owning a bar, I can make small talk with a rock if need be. As for this guy, I'll give him the time of day because it's the polite thing to do. But I hope he doesn't hang around for long. He's making me uneasy.

I exhale slowly, finding my resilience, like I've trained myself to do through meditation and yoga. To prepare myself and keep myself steady in situations like this one.

But it's written all over him: he's one of those rare people who has an animal power, you can feel it radiating off of him. Everyone in the room is aware of him, like he's a man-eating lion surveying his territory. In his presence, you feel yourself making a choice, to either make yourself available to him or get the hell out of his way. For my own sanity, I'm going with option two. "I work here and live here, so it all kind of blurs into one."

"What time does this place close?" He glances

around. The cling of his jacket as he moves shows off his gracefully burly muscles. He's tall and built but not in a gym-rat kind of way. It's more of a natural, born-this-way perfection.

"On a holiday weekend, we'll stay open as long as people want to drink," I tell him.

"Don't tell me you're working all night, Luna."

I glance at him warily. "How do you know my name?"

"Your friend called you that."

Wow. I'm well aware that the customer is always right, but it annoys me that he was listening in on my conversation with Josie. Some of that was intensely private information. He's not only penetrating barriers I don't want him inside of, he's also somehow knocking against my forcefield, ruffling me. My face is warm and I can feel my pulse in strange places. "Didn't anyone ever tell you eavesdropping is rude?"

"I wasn't eavesdropping." As if he wasn't smug enough, he folds his buff arms across his broad chest in the most beefcake way imaginable. A strand of his dark hair has fallen across his forehead, giving a softer edge to his extreme hotness. He's outrageously beautiful. And he knows it. "You happened to be having a conversation right in front of me. In a bar. I couldn't help overhearing some of it."

Anyway, it hardly matters. He'll be in town for the night or the weekend. He'll have a drink and disappear with this woman or another one and I'll never have to see him again.

I wish he would leave now.

Before that magnetic gaze does something to me I can't control.

I turn my attention to the next customer. "What can I get you, ma'am?" I ask the blond woman, who frowns at the word, like she's too young to be addressed that way. She must have bypassed thirty several years ago, but whatever. I quickly correct myself. "Er…miss? What would you like to drink?"

"I'll have a Sex on the Beach," she says, glancing at Mr. Smug.

Yikes.

She couldn't be any more obvious if she tried. But Mr. Smug doesn't seem all that interested, which makes the woman frown again, at least as much as her Botox fillers will allow.

"Coming right up," I say breezily. It's a bar, after all. It's where people try and fail and sometimes succeed at picking each other up. I watch a hundred scenes like this play out every day. Why should I care whether he gets laid tonight or not? I don't, is the answer to that question.

So I serve her drink and walk away. I can still feel the heat of his effect, like I've suddenly developed a light fever.

Don't look at him.

Do. Not. Look.

But I can't help it. I can feel that he's watching me.

Our eyes meet and—*oh, hell*—I blush.

I'm not scared of him. *I'm scared of how powerful his allure is, like freaking crack.*

To every woman in this room, I remind myself.

Mr. Smug has a drink with the blond. After a while she gets up to leave, looking unhappy about it.

So he's dismissed her.

The weekend crowd pours in and the bar gets busy. I'm thankful for the distraction. We have live music tonight, a jazz trio, and with the doors open and the moon on the water, I can't help but feel optimistic, despite Josie's pronouncement. Despite everything. Maybe she's right. Maybe this wasn't *our* dream all along. Maybe it was mine.

He's still watching me but I do my best to ignore him. With some distance, I feel my resolve returning and my self-preservation kicking in. It's hardly the first time a customer has offered to buy me a drink. So what if he's drop-dead gorgeous. Lots of people are.

Not that *drop-dead gorgeous.*

Even so, I brush him off as I get on with my job. I have no desire to be another notch on Casanova's bedpost. His dinner is served and he eats it at one of the tables out on the deck, scrolling on his phone, taking phone calls.

Rico and I are run off our feet for the next few hours and I'm relieved to notice the hot playboy is gone.

I can admit there might be fleeting pang of…*what, Luna? Regret? That you were borderline rude to him?*

No. No regrets. It's better this way.

A memory flits jarringly behind my brain. One of those ones I've triple-locked tightly into my box of hidden demons. I have no idea why it would be bubbling up now. I try to hold it back but it won't be held.

Come upstairs with me. There are some people I want you to meet.

Wow. Maybe I'm more tired than I realized. Maybe Josie and her situation are messing with my head more than I knew.

Meditation helps. I count to ten in my mind. I smile at a customer. I take an order.

By the time things start to slow down it's after midnight. I unload the last tray of glasses, using a clean dishtowel to polish the champagne flutes as I slide them back into the wine rack that hangs over the end of the bar.

"Is your shift over yet?"

I look up into a pair of ocean-blue eyes. "You're back."

"I like this place," he says. "It's got a good vibe to it."

"Thanks." But I refuse to be flattered by his cool charm. He's good, I've already acknowledged that. And I know better than to mess with the likes of him. He'll eat me for breakfast until all that's left is a bleached pile of bones.

Another chilling memory flutters through the recesses of my psyche.

Stop. Please. Please stop.

Come on, I saw you watching me. I could have any girl here tonight but I chose you. Consider yourself lucky.

Shit. Why is this happening? *Why now?*

"The view isn't bad, either," he adds as he continues to watch me. Mischief sparkles in his night-lit eyes.

He's sexy as hell. And if I don't keep my distance there's a very real chance I'll go with this.

Because I want to be whole again. I want to have fun and go wild and not have it turn into something that breaks your goddamn heart.

With him, it *would* be wild, you can just tell. It would be the wildest thing in the world.

Can I handle wild, is the question.

He's so muscular. Big. Heavy. Powerful enough to—

Damn it. I thought I was over all this stuff. "If that's a pick-up line, it should have died in the nineties."

He smiles at my reply. The humidity has made his hair curl lightly around his ears where it touches his collar, taking the edge off his businessman vibe. The shadow of his stubble is visible on his square jaw and his eyes are the color of stolen aquamarines. If you dressed him up differently, he could be a renegade gypsy king. There's something exotic about him.

How many women would this man have clocked up

over the course of his sex life? I can't help wondering. A hundred? Several hundred? A thousand?

Has he ever done things they didn't want him to do?

"Ready for that drink yet?" He's wearing a different shirt. A navy blue polo shirt, which makes the color of his eyes even more striking. He probably keeps an extra in his bag for all those glasses of wine that get thrown in his face. He must have checked into his hotel and come back for a nightcap. "When does the night shift take over?"

Jimmy walks through the door. "Here he is now." We tend to get a steady stream of visitors into the small hours of the morning, especially on holidays. A lot of people drink their way through Thanksgiving and Christmas, for whatever reason. I get it. It's something I'm tempted to do myself. My father will be happily ensconced in his Westchester McMansion with his new family, his *better* family, the one he didn't walk out on and who were willing turn a blind eye to his extracurricular activities. My mother will be misery-pounding apple martinis with her old, ugly sugar daddy.

I wonder what this guy's reason is. What he's running from or trying to avoid. "No family get-together back in Connecticut to rush home to?" I say blithely, serving him another Jack Daniels on ice and pouring myself a rum and Coke. I *will* take a risk again one day, but not today. There's enough upheaval in my immediate future to deal with already. One drink before bed then I'll head upstairs and see how Josie is doing.

"Chicago, actually," he says. "And no." He takes a sip of his drink, watching me in that relaxed, confident, hyper-alert way. "What about you? Not heading home to Iowa this year?"

I meet his gaze. "Wow, you really did listen in to our —clearly not that it matters to you—private conversation."

He barely shrugs, non-repentantly. His perfect mouth quirks. "As I said, I was innocently enjoying a drink and couldn't help but overhear. Sounds like you've got a small problem."

I'm tired. I'm scared of what might happen over the next few weeks. I'm not in the mood for his playful scorn. His alpha male aura is messing with my calm, mostly-stable outlook. There's an edge to my well-trained polite-ness that isn't polite at all. "I'm not sure that's any of your business. Besides, shouldn't you be shacked up with your harem by now? It's late."

His not-quite-smile is more amused than offended. He traces his finger around the rim of his glass but his eyes are still on me. His hands are tan and strong-looking. "I'm not in the mood for my harem tonight."

Is that a joke? I shake my head lightly as I slide the last flute into place. "That's surprising."

"I guess I should be flattered you think I'd be up to the task."

I feel a flush rise to my cheeks as I can't help picturing him *up to the task*. I have no doubt he would be very much up to the task and the thought sends a surge of awareness through me. His self-assured charisma, his obvious athleticism and his raw masculinity make it kind of obvious that *oh, God, I do. I want to know what it would be like to feel* good. *To feel loved instead of—*

No. I'm deluding myself.

He's a playboy. Obviously. He's exactly what I've been running from. A textbook example of what to avoid at all costs. What I need is to find myself someone who's less threatening, who doesn't scare me, who calms me and won't try to control me.

"I'm Gage," he says. "Gage McCabe."

The name sounds vaguely familiar to me, but I have no idea why it would. I finish my drink and place the empty glass in one of the dishwasher trays. "And I'm going to bed. Goodnight, Mr. McCabe. Happy Thanksgiving."

"Have dinner with me tomorrow night."

Casanova is persistent. "I'm working tomorrow night."

"On Thanksgiving?"

"It's one of our busiest days."

"Friday night, then."

I've already decided I'm not going anywhere near this guy, as to-die-for as he may be. He's got hot sex and heartbreak written all over him, and as much as I might crave one of the above—*more and more, as though urges of my body are on overdrive even as they clash violently with the voices in my head*—I can't deal with the combination. "Also one of our busiest days. The whole weekend is basically mayhem. You have a good night now."

With that, I leave him to his drink. As I close the door to the stairs of my apartment behind me, I glance back at his face. There's a determination there I don't like the look of.

I check on Josie, who's fast asleep. I take a long shower to wash off the day and I collapse into bed, hoping tomorrow isn't the beginning of the end of everything I've worked so hard for.

Gage McCabe.

Where have I heard that name before? And why does my brain keep retracing the lines of his face, the intense look in his eyes and that raw, dark-edged magnetism…

…which promises only a world of trouble.

Go on, girl. Get some of that angst out of your system. Take the risk. Replace the bad memories with a few good ones. You know he'd take you on a wild ride. Live a little.

Once again, I scuttle the devil-voice in my head forcefully back into her cage. I'm living enough. I've got a business to save, a best friend jumping ship on our lifelong dream because she has no choice, and a very busy weekend ahead of me.

With any luck, Mr. Smug—*Gage McCabe*—will be gone by morning.

Before I can recall where I might have read about him or why, I'm fast asleep.

6

———

GAGE

I SEE HER STANDING THERE, on the other side of the room. I recognize this place. We're in the convention center downtown. It's crowded. It's one of those fundraisers, with dozens of round tables set up for dinner. There are decorations and a stage with a podium for the speakers and the presentations. Everyone is dressed in black.

Except for her.

She's wearing her yellow dress.

She looks out of place. She's glittery and sunlit as though a bright ray of sun shines only on her. She's lightly tanned and her hair is barely windblown, like she might have just stepped inside after spending the afternoon running through the summer fields of Iowa. I can smell her scent from here, of ripe wheat and roses and sweet, sweet perfection.

She lights up the room. She is, quite literally, the sun.

Someone touches my shoulder. I brush them off. I can't take my eyes off the girl in the yellow dress and I don't want to. I want to look at her and no one else. I'm crazy-thirsty, to drink in the sight of her. I want more.

I need to get closer.

She sees me.

She smiles at me.

Her smile infuses me with a strange kind of longing. And happiness. The emotion surges through me jarringly. When's the last time I experienced pure, undiluted happiness? I can't remember.

I try to walk toward her but I can't. I'm swimming against a forceful tide. People are slowing me down. They're holding my arms. It's that woman who stole my cuff links whose name I can't remember. And others. Grabbing for me.

How dare they! A boiling rage overcomes me.

With primal effort, I break free of them.

But Luna's walking away.

I'm running, trying with everything I have to get closer to her.

I want her. I call out to her.

She turns.

At the far side of the room, where she's standing, the scene is changing. There's a sandy beach and an ocean at sunset, opening out to an infinite horizon. She pulls off her yellow dress.

I can't breathe.

She's wearing a yellow bikini.

She's the air and the water and the sun. She's my thirst and my hunger.

Her body is so insanely exquisite, I can't bear it. I'm going mad. I want to put my mouth on her. I want to eat her and drink her and suck on her. I'll die if I don't, I'm certain of this.

She laughs at me but it's a cute laugh. An inviting laugh.

I look down to see what she's laughing at.

My jacket and my white shirt are open. My chest is bloody. For some reason, I don't mind this. I'm much more concerned about my cock. Inside my pants—barely—I'm painfully huge and hard. I need her, now. The fever of my lust is unbearable. I need to be inside her. I need to come inside her.

She's oxygen and light. She's beauty and cool, hot relief.

The agony is both physical and existential. I need to taste her and absorb her. I need to be on her and in her.

What the hell is happening to me?

Gage, she says.

She's holding something in her hands.

What is it?

I walk closer to her. A warm wave washes over our feet.

I want to kiss her mouth. I need to devour her.

I lean closer. Please, please let me.

She offers me the thing she's holding in her hands but I don't want it. I want to kiss her mouth.

Take it, she says.

I don't want to take it. I just want to taste her mouth.

Take it back, she insists.

No, I say. I don't want it. It's yours.

I look down to see what it is.

It's bloody.

The blood is dripping from her hands.

I realize then that she's holding my beating heart.

I JERK AWAKE.

Fuck.

Where am I?

I sit up and put my hands on my chest to feel for blood. There's none. I'm intact. There's no hole there. My heart is still inside me and it's beating fast.

Fucking hell.

My cock is as engorged and painful as it was in the dream. It's heavy and hot and hard as a fucking pillar of granite.

I'm in a hotel. The executive suite of a five-star resort. In Key West. I remember now.

Luna.

The sassy little bartender.

Fuck, I was dreaming about her.

It was so vivid. It's *still* so vivid.

I lay back on the bed.

I take my cock in my fist, carefully. I'm so hard and bursting, it hurts.

Slowly, I slide my fist along my thick length.

I close my eyes and return to my dreamscape. I don't care about my heart. This time I can control what happens here. This time I don't have to wait. I can take whatever I want of her. I pick her up and lay her down carefully on the soft sand. I begin to devour her. I lick into her mouth and rip off her bikini. I suck on her cherry-ripe nipples that taste like candy. She laughs that inviting laugh. She's wet for me. I can't wait any longer. I need to be inside her. I slide my cock deep and—*oh, fucking fuck fuck fuck*—I come harder than I ever have in my life. All over my stomach and chest, my cum spurts from my cock in hot, excruciating bursts.

I'm breathing hard.

I'm sweating. I left the sliding door of the balcony open last night and it's hot in here.

My heartbeat feels more meaningful than usual. I'm aware of a light, transcendent ache with each beat, like it's still bleeding. Like it remembers the echoing grasp of her cool hands.

I hear my own low oath.

This is fucking crazy.

Why am I dreaming about her?

Why do I feel all twisted and fucked up?

I get out of bed. There's no way I can sleep. I'm sticky and sweaty and pissed off. I just came hard but I want to come again.

I check the time. It's 3:08 a.m.

It's too early to go to the gym or for a swim. I need to do something with this raging energy. I pace for a while. I could take a cold shower but I don't want to.

I don't want to wash her away yet.

She got me sticky and wet. She *did this.*

But why?

Why her?

Why am I dreaming and now obsessing about *her*, of all people?

Because she brushed me off, probably. It's been a long time since a woman did that to me, the little minx. It's the conquest that's got me riled up, that's all.

You have a good night now. I'll goodnight you, sweetheart.

The angelic bartender who wants nothing to do with me.

We'll see about that.

If she didn't already have my attention with her feisty attitude and her nymphet face and that crazy-sweet body, she sure has it now.

What she doesn't realize is that ignoring me is roughly the equivalent of waving a red flag at a feral two-ton bull. Even my subconscious won't let that slide. So she's invading my dreams. Fine. I've dealt with that. *In my dreams I've possessed her. I've come deep inside her tight, squeezing pussy.*

Now all I need to do is fuck her in real life.

I'll be a lot more thorough. I'll suck on her nipples until she moans. I'll eat her pussy until she's coming on my tongue. I'll drive her crazy with lust like she's doing to me now. Then I'll thrust deep inside her until her orgasm milks the hot cum from my cock in seedy bursts.

I'm fully hard again. *Fucking hell.* Harder than hard. Throbbing and hot.

I want her, in a way that's messing with my head.

And what I want, I get. The fact that she's playing hard to get is…cute. And for some reason, hot as fuck.

I don't know if a woman has *ever* played hard to get with me, come to think of it.

Luckily I have an ace up my sleeve.

She handed me the keys to her life without even meaning to. The little honey is in a bind and needs a bail out.

The thing is, I play hardball. I don't fuck around, especially when I want something—some*one*—this badly. I can't remember this ever happening before. I go after businesses and investments like this: with singular focus that no one and nothing can distract me from. But not women. I don't need to chase them. They lay at my feet. They offer before I've even asked.

Except one, so it seems.

Sassy, gorgeous Luna from Iowa, of all people, is the one who's gotten under my skin.

Holding my bloody, beating heart in her hands.

That was just a dream, I remind myself. A nightmare, more accurately.

I take my laptop out of my bag and open it.

I do some preliminary due diligence and send a few emails.

Then I google her.

She doesn't have much of a digital footprint. A Facebook account. *Luna LaRoux.* A very light Instagram with a few pictures of sunsets. *@lunalarouxxx*

Mine. Those x's are mine.

Gage, you need to get a goddamn grip, son.

There's an article about her business dated almost a year ago, when the two of them took over ownership of the restaurant. There's a photo of Luna and Josie behind the bar.

Damn, she's pretty. She looks young and happy.

Like she did in the dream.

I want to make her smile like that.

My heart does that thing again where I'm aware of its bloody, heavy rhythm.

I close my laptop.

It's not enough.

I need more.

I lay back on the bed. I close my eyes and I think of her. In her yellow dress. Behind the bar. On the dream beach. I peel off her clothes more slowly this time, tasting every inch of that flawless skin. I kiss my way down her body. *To her pussy. God, I want to taste her so much.*

The fantasy is too much. I come hard and fast. Even harder than the first time. Harder and longer and more forcefully, like my cock is on super-powered overdrive.

Fuck. This is bad.

I lay there panting in the dark, covered in my own sweat and cum. My blood feels hot and rabid. Like an animal. That's how I feel. Like a hungry, out-of-control wild animal who knows what it wants. *An alpha beast who's caught the scent. Who's on the hunt now and can't be tamed. Watch out, Luna LaRoux. You have no idea what you're in for.*

I open my eyes and stare at the ceiling.

Christ, Gage. What the fuck?

I take a deep breath, wiping myself with the sheet, trying like hell to calm the fuck down.

But it's no use. My fantasies turn dark and I let them.

Much later, I finally succumb to sleep and the perfect surrender of her sweet, beautiful mouth.

7

GAGE

I sleep deeply and when I wake again it's 6:37.

What a nightmare I had.

I get up and wrap a towel around my waist. *Fuck, I'm a mess.*

My suite has a balcony that looks out over the pool and out to the beach beyond. I step out onto it and vaguely take in the view. People in white shirts are setting up loungers and blue umbrellas.

Then I go inside and take a long, much-needed shower. I order room service and check my emails. There are already a couple of replies. My investigators know I'll pay whatever they ask so they'll jump through hoops for me and work all night.

The girls' names are Josie Farrell and Luna LaRoux. Both hail from the outskirts of Cedar Rapids, Iowa, where Josie's father owned a small building business that was sold after he died. Her mother died when she was young. She has three brothers who all still live in their hometown.

Luna's family is more difficult to trace. My phone rings again and it's Pete Clancy, the guy I use when I want hard-to-reach information about people. "Her parents divorced when she was six," he says. "Up until then, she'd lived at their family home in Scarsdale, a modest three-bedroom ranch house that was sold when the divorce went through. The father remarried two weeks after the divorce papers were signed. He has two young children with his former secretary. He's a lawyer but has been cited once for misconduct which got him demoted from partner and almost cost him his job. He recently made a couple of bad investments. His new house in Rye is mortgaged to the hilt. He uses a separate credit card under an alias to book his hotel rooms by the hour—several a week. Luna's mother remarried several times and now lives in Los Angeles with her fourth husband, who runs a struggling movie studio. In the minutes of the studio's last board meeting, filing for bankruptcy was discussed. The mother is currently doing her fourth stint in rehab for alcohol abuse. From what I can tell, there's not much of a relationship between Luna and her mother. Luna's last phone call to California was four months ago. That's all I've got so far, but I'll keep tracking and get back to you."

"Don't bother," I tell him, even though I'm not sure why. Digging behind her back feels invasive, maybe. I'd rather she tells me herself instead. Not my usual style, but maybe it's just Key West having its way with me again.

If all goes according to plan, she'll be telling me her life story by the end of happy hour.

And I found out what I needed to know. She has no Plan B. No parents to call on and ask for money, since the relationships are frayed and they're both financially hanging on by the skin of their teeth.

It's a beautiful morning, sunny and hot and hazy.

I make a point of toning down my dream hangover. It was intense and I still feel dazed.

I try not to analyze it, aside from the way her dream body felt under mine. *As I came hard inside her.*

I try not to fixate on the blaring metaphor that it doesn't take a shrink to point out. *She was literally holding your heart in her hands. What does that mean? Does your subconscious think you're fucking in love with her or something? After one glance and a brief, dismissive conversation?*

I almost laugh at myself.

Pathetic.

It's true that people in my family tend to fall hard. My parents did and now both my brothers seem to be suffering from the same affliction.

Good thing I'm immune to that kind of bullshit. I dodged that bullet. I've already acknowledged that I'm incapable of love. This weird meltdown is only because she didn't fall in lust with me at first glance, like women always do. I'm not used to Luna's reaction, that's all this is. This is just a small bruise to my ego, which I plan on fixing pronto.

I have a plan. I'm bored with my usual investment portfolio. Dealing day in and day out with stiff suits and greasy bankers. I feel like mixing it up.

And showing her who's boss.

Answering her brazen little come-backs.

Shouldn't you be shacked up with your harem by now? It's late.

I'll show the little sweetheart the true meaning of *shacked up* and then some.

I arrive at the Sea Breeze just after ten. I'm glad to see Josie out on the deck, setting the tables. I'm not sure if it's possible, but she looks even more pregnant this morning than she did last night. She glances up at me and her jaw drops slightly. It's a typical reaction. In fact the only woman who *hasn't* reacted to me like that lately is the lippy nymphet who's going to be in my bed by sunset, if I get my way—which I always do.

"Ms. Farrell, I'm Gage McCabe. I have a business proposition I'd like to discuss with you and your business partner."

Her eyes do that thing they all do. Travel. Check me out. Notice there's nothing commonplace about me. I'm grade A prime beef and women always take a few seconds to absorb the extent of it. That's just the way it is.

"What kind of business proposition?"

"I'd prefer to discuss that with both of you together, if you don't mind. Do you have a few minutes?"

"Does this have anything to do with the sale of the bar?"

"Yes. As a matter of fact it does."

"How do you know about that?" Josie asks. "We haven't advertised yet."

"I couldn't help overhearing some of your conversation yesterday. And Luna filled me in on a few of the details last night." Not particularly willingly, but I don't bother mentioning that part.

"Oh."

"Is she available now?"

"Uh…I'll text her. She's upstairs doing yoga." She pulls her phone out of her apron.

Damn it. The thought of Luna in tight little exercise clothes, *how flexible she probably is, sweaty and barely clothed and…*fucking hell. The last thing I need is a raging hard-on for our impromptu business meeting. I try to think of baseball and grandmothers—anything—to ease the rising tide, when I see a pumped-up gym rat walking up the stairs that lead to the deck from the small beach. His tight t-shirt says Go Out With Me Luna.

What?

No.

Luna's going to go out with *me*, that's the way this is going to play out, fucker.

I'm glaring at the guy as he strolls past, giving me a what's-up flick of his eyebrows. "Hey, Josie," he says.

"Hey, Kyle. This is, um…sorry, what was your name again?"

"Gage McCabe."

The kid's eyebrows shoot up. "No shit! Dude, I read about you in GQ! You're that investment guru. And July's style icon."

It's times like these I regret the magazine spreads and their ridiculous articles about my fucking "style," whatever that is. I wear clothes I happen to like and that fit me, that's about as far as my style goes.

"Would you be able to give me some investment pointers?" asks the dipshit. "I've been playing around with a couple of ideas…" I can barely concentrate on what he's saying. Would Luna really consider going out with this guy? What's the meaning of his t-shirt? What are the intricacies of her relationship with him?

And why the fuck am I getting so worked up about this?

It's a question that's answered as soon as Luna walks onto the deck, which happens at that precise moment.

She's dressed in—exactly as I pictured—tight workout clothes. Her hair has been pulled back into a high ponytail but shorter pieces frame her face and are damp with sweat. Her cheeks are pink with health and vitality and her body is like something straight out of a fucking wet dream. *Even better than the wet dream.* She's long-limbed and slim but curvy. Her smooth skin is gleaming. She's toned but at the same time soft-looking in such a feminine, luscious kind of a way, all I can think about is *what she would feel like*. I've fantasized but I don't actually *know*. I want to feast on her gorgeousness like I've never wanted anything in my entire debauched, wretched goddamn life.

I hold my leather briefcase in front of me. I try to look casual about it but there's nothing casual about my hard-on. It's gargantuan and as agonizing as it was last night.

Baseball baseball baseball.

But it's useless. Even baseball won't save me at this point.

How does she do *that?*

She doesn't look happy to see me.

She doesn't look happy to see Kyle either. At least I can take heart in *that* detail.

"Kyle," she says, pissed off. "Can you stop with the t-shirt? Take it off."

Kyle grins at her and peels off his shirt, showing off his weird muscles, which makes me want to punch him in the face. I almost do it.

What the fuck is wrong with me? I am absolutely on the verge of tackling this douchebag to the ground and pummeling his face with my fist.

Luna doesn't appear to find Kyle's muscles as impressive as he clearly finds them. "Go inside and put on one of the merch t-shirts," she says.

"Do they come in extra-extra-large?" dumbass asks. "'Cause that's the only size that will fit me."

Fucking hell.

Luna looks mildly repulsed, I'm happy to notice.

Kyle slings his t-shirt over his shoulder. "I heard the Tucker Brothers Band is playing at a secret location in Key West tomorrow night. My friend might be able to get me tickets."

At this, Luna's eyes light up. "The Tucker Brothers? Really? Oh, I love them."

My torment is three-headed at this point. A) She loves their *music*, like millions of people do, that's all. And am I *jealous*? Is that what this enraged, rip-their-hearts-out feeling is? B) I'm already so hot for this girl with her beatific face and ludicrously perfect body in its skimpy little sweat-dampened yoga outfit, my cock is on red-hot overdrive and I'm seriously struggling to conceal it, and C) she's glaring at me like I'm somehow even worse than the muscle-bound dipshit over here who's in the middle of asking her out on a date, which she's clearly considering.

"I've got tickets," I hear myself say. "VIP seats. They're my cousins."

"The Tuckers are your cousins?" Luna asks.

This pisses me off even more. I don't need my goddamn *cousins* to get me a date.

"Aww, man," says Kyle. "Can you get *me* a VIP seat?"

"No."

Luna's still staring at me. "What are you doing here? It's a little early for whiskey, isn't it?" Not exactly welcoming.

This doesn't worry me. I'll thaw her out. I just need some time with her, to give her a chance to succumb to my charms, like they all inevitably do.

Josie lowers herself into a chair, holding her round stomach. "He wants to discuss a business proposal with us."

Luna looks at Josie, then back at me. "What kind of business proposal?"

I pin a glare on Kyle. "Would you excuse us?"

He gives me a blank look, then wanders away, thank fuck.

"What did he mean when he said you're an investment guru?" Josie asks.

"Ladies, if you'll sit down with me for a few minutes, I'll explain exactly what my offer is." Keeping my leather briefcase strategically in front of me, I take a seat. I pull out an envelope and place it on the table.

Luna makes no move to sit.

What I have in mind is riding on Josie, so I slide the envelope toward her. "Your business, including real estate, as well as existing structures, fixtures and chattels, is valued at one point one million dollars. According to records—which are all public, by the way—you owe a total of one million and thirty-five thousand dollars, which gives you an equity of sixty-five thousand dollars, divided in half, more or less. I wasn't eavesdropping," –a glare from Luna— "but I did happen to overhear, Josie, that you own fifty-one percent of the business, which would mean that you personally own thirty-three thousand, one hundred and fifty dollars of equity."

"Um…yes."

"I'd like to buy out your share for four hundred thousand dollars."

Josie blinks at me. "What?"

"That's my offer, but it rides on me retaining the majority share. I'm not willing to negotiate for less."

"But that's far more than it's worth," Josie points out.

"Yes." Which is the only way Luna will ever agree to it, because Josie is desperate and this will solve all—or at least most—of her problems. "I see good potential in this business. I think there's a lot more you could do with it. You could expand the deck into a destination with a much larger seating area. We could retain the character of the place, spruce it up and build on it. I have a yacht we could offer as a special event charter. There's a potential to expand the event calendar, too, with big name musicians and so on. I can discuss it with my cousins. I'm sure I can talk them into being our first headline act. If the deal goes ahead, that is."

"No," Luna says.

Josie gives her a shocked are-you-crazy glare.

"Josie could consider that offer for forty-nine percent," Luna continues. "And we'd need to discuss how involved you'd be in the business."

I meet Luna's green gaze levelly. She's fucking heartbreaking. Even sweaty and pink-faced from her work-out she's stunningly pretty. It's weirdly painful and hypnotic to look at her. "As I said, the fifty-one percent is non-negotiable." I anticipated Luna's hesitation. And I want this deal airtight. It's not about the money, which I have so much of at this point I can easily afford to pay whatever it takes. So I play my next card. "But you're right, maybe I've bid too low. Let's make it six hundred thousand for Josie's fifty-one percent. As far as my involvement goes, I'm planning on spending the next month in Key West." *Am I?* Yes. I am. I need to get my fill, and this time it's going to take longer than one night. *That body. That face.* Call me a deviant, I don't care. I want her. She's lit some kind of fucking bonfire in me that wants to be fed. "After that, I'll be going back to Chicago."

I have a fleeting thought that maybe…Luna will want to come with me.

What the fuck are you thinking, you asshole? You don't sleep with women more than once, remember? You'll have moved on by the end of the weekend. What are you even doing right now?

"Did you say *six hundred thousand dollars?*" Josie murmurs. She has tears in her eyes, with relief, maybe.

Luna, however, has daggers shooting out of hers. "Why do you even want to buy into this business? That's a crazy offer. I don't trust you, Mr. —"

"Gage." I try and barely succeed in holding back a wolfish grin—because I'm experienced enough to know when an offer is going to be accepted, even if it takes a little coercion—which I realize isn't helping. She doesn't trust me. And so she shouldn't. "This could be a very profitable business. And I can help you take it there. Once it's been refurbished and we've realized its full potential, I'll go home to Chicago and you can be rid of me but still get the use of all my money."

"You decided all this when you 'overheard' our conversation yesterday?" Using air quotes with her fingers. The sprinkling of freckles across Luna's nose gives me an odd craving. The color of her mouth infuses me with an unfamiliarly fanatical kind of lust that makes my heart lurch hotly.

Like it was when she was holding it in her hands.

But I somehow keep my cool, aside from one rock-hard detail. "Yes. As I said, I can see the potential. I'm an investor. I'm always on the lookout for businesses that are being underutilized."

"Underutilized?" Luna says the word like I've insulted her. She pulls up one of the chairs and sits. I can smell her lightly perfumed scent, of flowers and fantasies I want to live inside. *Just like I imagined, but far, far better because she's real and sitting here right next to me.* "What kind of investor are you?" As she bites gently on her plump bottom lip, my hard-on throbs painfully.

Fucking hell.

This is bad.

Very, very bad. "A successful one. My father taught me and my brothers when we were young, so I've had a lot of practice. I've bought and sold dozens of businesses. I know a diamond in the rough when I see one."

Luna tucks a strand of hair behind her ear. Even her ears are perfect. *I'll gently take the soft flesh of her earlobe between my teeth. I'll lick and kiss her neck before thrusting my tongue into her luscious mouth.*

Christ.

Her eyes narrow. "What's your motive, Mr. McCabe?"

"My motive? There's no motive, aside from making money, which I think we could, if we make the much-needed upgrades."

"The answer is still no." If looks could kill I'd be a bloody pulp on the floor right now.

Why is it that one woman I've *really* wanted—not just because I feel like getting laid but because she's *Luna*—doesn't want anything to do with me? Is this some kind of twisted karmic retribution coming back to bite me in the ass after years of not giving a fuck about anything or anyone?

Strange things always happen to me around this time of year. My parents' memories rev into high gear and mess with the usual rhythm of my life. That Luna just so happened to walk into my life this weekend is fucked-up but not surprising. Like they're lecturing me from the afterlife to settle down and aim higher in the one area of my life I can admit I'm less than scrupulous.

The thought riles me, for one reason, and probably

not the reason it should: will going to bed with Luna once or twice or several times over the course of the weekend cure me of this sudden *thing* that's happening to me? This bizarre obsession and the erotic-sweet nightmares and the ferocious, feral lust I'm suddenly mired in?

Yes.

No.

I don't know.

Fuck.

"The answer is maybe," Josie says.

"*If* we split fifty-fifty," Luna insists. "That's our final offer."

The plans I have require a majority share, and I know Luna will cave because she'll be thinking first about her friend's best interests. Luna is stubborn. She doesn't lack courage at all, that's obvious, but their financial situation is teetering on a knife's edge. Marlon their guarantor—and I know from one of the emails I received this morning that he's Josie's older brother—must have some serious equity. Probably from the family compound back in Iowa. Most banks wouldn't lend this much without at least some capital behind them to spend on maintenance and operations. However all that played out, I can see that Josie is Luna's Achilles heel, her one weakness. "As I said, the majority share is non-negotiable."

More daggers. The cutest, sexiest goddamn daggers I've ever seen.

Why am I suddenly so fascinated by this angry, standoffish little woman?

Possibly because she's the most stunningly beautiful *angry, standoffish little woman in the history of my world.*

And I can't let her slip through my fingers because I didn't push hard enough. I want her where I want her and I'm prepared to do whatever it takes to put her there. This goes against every grain of business sense I possess—which is a shitload—but I hear myself saying, "Fifty-one percent for one million dollars. That's my final offer."

Josie's pink cheeks pale, which is mildly concerning. "*A million dollars?*" she squeaks.

Luna exhales a sigh that's somewhere between disbelief and defeat. Josie hears it, and glances at her friend. There's empathy in Josie's expression and for a split second I feel a pang of something that might be… compassion? It's hard to identify because it doesn't show up on my radar all that often. Or ever, to be precise.

I'm giving them no choice. I'm bullying the situation, like I so often do. Why do I suddenly feel sort of bad about it?

I'm *helping* them, I remind myself. I'm setting Josie up with enough money to raise her children comfortably, without any financial worries.

To get to Luna.

To get with Luna.

To get Luna into your bed.

So?

Is that so bad? I can do what I want with my money. It's *my* money, for fuck's sake.

Josie attempts to get to her feet, but it takes some effort. I stand up to help her, desperately trying to keep my rampant hard-on concealed.

Josie picks up the envelope. "Mr. Mc—"

"Gage."

"Gage." Josie smiles gently, and I already know I've won. "It's a generous offer and we appreciate it. But we're going to need some time to talk it through."

"Take all the time you need."

"Can we meet with you tomorrow?" Josie asks.

"Of course." It's disappointing, that Luna won't be in my bed *tonight*, but twenty-four hours will give me enough time to plan my next move so thoroughly Luna will have no choice but to surrender to me. "You two talk it over. How about I meet with both of you here tomorrow afternoon around five and you can let me know what you've decided. After that," I add, smiling at Luna—genuinely, because she's gorgeous and it's making me stupidly happy for reasons I can't control or entirely understand— "I'll take you to my cousins' gig. Both of you, if you'd like." Because Luna is more likely to agree if it doesn't feel like a date. And Josie will refuse.

"A night on the town is more than I can handle in my current state." Josie pats her round stomach. "Besides, Luna's more of a Tucker Brothers Band fan than me. Are they really your cousins?"

It's pissing me off to no end that I'm resorting to using fucking Travis, Vaughn and Kade to get myself a date, but I've already decided I'll do whatever it takes. "Yes. So what do you say?" There's a hopefulness in my voice I don't even recognize. "It'll be fun."

Fun? You sound like a fucking imbecile.

I don't care. I'll convince her I'm not a bully or a jerk. For the first time in a very long time, I actually care about what another person thinks of me. I want her to…*like* me. Go figure.

Clearly, not only does she *not* like me, she loathes me. This is obvious by the fury shining out of her jewel-bright eyes. "No," she says. "I don't think so. I'm busy tomorrow night."

Josie stares at her friend sharply. "But you *love* the Tucker Brothers. We have plenty of staff on tomorrow night, Luna. You should totally go. It'll give you two a chance to talk about everything and to start making plans."

"We haven't decided the sale will go ahead yet," Luna says. She's surly.

"The seats are front row," I add. "We'll have a drink with the band before the show."

Luna's glaring at me, as though she's not sure she loves the band enough to put up with *me* for an entire evening. Judging by the cocktail of emotion coloring her expression, ranging from hatred to annoyance to rage—to something else, buried deeper, which is harder to read—

I've got my work cut out for me. And I can hardly wait. I've spent a lifetime building my arsenal. Of seduction, of money, of buying whatever I want.

I don't want to buy her.

I have this unfamiliar urge to fucking *win* her.

She sighs. "Fine," she finally says.

Yes!

I'll show her. I can be a good person, she'll see.

I don't always use people to get what I want.

She'll fall in lust with me. She has to.

Maybe even in love. Once she discovers the things I can do.

I'll have her right where I want her.

Under me. Submitting. Taking me inside.

Hell, yeah.

She'll see.

Fuck.

8

———

"I CAN'T BELIEVE that jerk! Who does he think he *is*? Waltzing in here offering a million freaking *dollars*? I mean, what the hell? Who would *do* that, just out of the blue? He's a total stranger who doesn't know the first thing about us or our business!"

We're upstairs and Josie is sitting on the couch, leafing through the contract. I spent a fitful, sleepless night. Even an extra-intense yoga practice this morning couldn't cure me of all the pent-up frustration. My life has just changed irrevocably, and all because of one ego-maniacal playboy who won't even consider less than fifty-one percent.

"You're pacing," she says. "Actually, he seems to know a whole lot about our business, down to the exact amount of money we owe."

"Exactly. How does a person even find out about details like that?"

"He said a lot of it was public information."

"But not *all* of it! Our bank statements? Our equity? The value of our damn *chattels*? That's the kind of detail he would have had to go to our bank to find out about. Which is a very devious and underhanded way to go about something like this."

More leafing. "Or…maybe it's the sensible and informed way to go about something like this? Just sayin'. He's offering to buy our business. It's not unreasonable for him to want to find out about its value."

"Behind our backs? That's asshole behavior!"

"It's savvy investor behavior, Luna. I don't know why you're getting so worked up about this. It's what we wanted, remember? We would've had to provide all that information to any investor. He's clearly well-connected, so what? Now we don't have to go through all the trouble of advertising and vetting people and scrambling around to get the best possible offer. We've just had the best damn offer we're ever likely to get."

"But why would he offer *so much*? It doesn't make any sense for him to do that." I stare out at the view of the sun on the water and…I don't want to leave this place. I don't want to go back to Iowa with its landlocked endlessness. I love the ocean views and the sea salt and the humid warmth. I love this place with everything I have. "I don't trust that prick as far as I can throw him."

"Really? I couldn't tell." Josie smiles sympathetically. "As he said, he can see the potential in our business. You should be *happy*, Luna. He's an experienced businessman who's willing to sink a ton of money into this place, which is exactly what it needs. What's the problem?"

"His ego could be assigned its own zip code, that's the problem. I want to know what he's up to."

"Why do you think he's 'up to' anything? Maybe he legitimately thinks this business is worth taking to the next level. We always saw the potential. Maybe he can too."

I sit down on the couch next to Josie. "He's obviously a power-hungry control freak."

She's smiling again. "He's also hot as fuck, honey. And ridiculously loaded. I can think of worse business partners. Look at this, I just googled him. He's some kind of bigshot. He owns entire buildings in Chicago. You have to interview with him to buy into his investment company. He probably takes over businesses every day of the week."

I glance at Josie's laptop. There's a photo of Gage, standing next to a yacht. Looking just as self-important as always. "I'm not interested in being owned. Especially by him."

"He won't own *you*. He'll own half of the business."

"More than half. I mean, why is he so insistent on the fifty-one percent?"

"Because it makes business sense, I hate to say it. By the way, did you happen see the way he was looking at you?" She elbows me playfully.

"No."

"Sweetie," she says gently, "It was a long time ago now. Water under the bridge at this point. Don't you think it might be time to move on—"

"Don't, Josie. Please."

Thankfully, she refrains from expanding on the deep dark details about my past I *really* don't want to talk about right now. She sighs, but backs off. An unspoken under-standing passes between us. She knows everything about my backstory. She's the one who was there for me and who talked me off the ledge when everything fell apart. She knows why I hate people like Gage McCabe. The kind of men who think they own the world and don't care how much damage they inflict or how much wreckage they leave behind. "Fine," she says. "But I think you should look at it objectively. He's offering to help you fix this place up and turn it into everything you always dreamed it could be, before he then disappears back to his penthouse in Chicago. We really couldn't ask for anything better."

"As far as I'm concerned he can take his million dollars and stick it."

"Yes. Right into my bank account." Josie laughs at her own joke, but her expression softens. "Loon, I won't sell it to him if you don't want me to. We'll just tell him no and we can run the advertisement like we were planning to. Who knows, someone else might offer even more."

We both know that's never going to happen.

She exhales a sudden breath and places both her

hands on her swollen belly. "*Luna.* I just felt the babies kick!"

She places my palm on her stomach and I feel it too. Wow.

The fluttery movement is as life-affirming as anything has ever been. It makes me feel sad and happy and at the same time hopeful. "Oh, Josie," I whisper.

Of course I know what I'm going to do. I can bitch and moan as much as I want to about my new business partner-to-be. But I'm going to do the right thing by my best friend. We're going to accept the offer so she can go home to Iowa and never have to worry about money or health insurance or buying enough food and clothes and even college funds for her beautiful children.

"We're not going to tell him no."

Josie looks at me hopefully. "We're not?"

"No. We're not. We're going to tell him yes."

Tears well up in her eyes. "But are you sure? I don't want to do it unless you're happy with the arrangement, Loon. And you're not happy, I can see that."

"I'm happy that *you're* happy. I'll be fine. I'll bleed Gage McCabe dry and the bar will be fantastic and the Tucker Brothers Band will play here and we'll be the most popular place in all of Key West. I can handle him."

Can I?

I'll *have* to handle him. Because it's my bar and it's my life. And I definitely don't want some arrogant bastard trying to run it.

"I wish I didn't have to leave you," Josie says.

I think about trying to convince her to stay, again. But I don't. "You're going to have a great life with your family and your babies in Iowa. As soon as your plane touches down on that Iowa dirt, you're going to feel like you're home."

"Yeah," she smiles sort of sadly. "I think maybe you're right."

No matter how much I might dislike Gage McCabe and everything he stands for—greed, power, *raunchy and meaningless sex*—at least I know I'm doing the right thing. At least I'll know that Josie will be well taken care of.

Josie wipes her eyes. "Are you sure you don't want to come with me? We could offer the whole thing to Mr. Swish Investor and he could take it off our hands and you could come live with me in Iowa."

As much as I loathe the idea of being Gage McCabe's minority-share business partner, I don't want to give up on my life and my hopes. "I can't go back to Iowa. I get why you'd want to. It's where you come from and where you were always going to end up. But not me."

"I know, Loon. And I know things will work out for you here. It really is a good deal he's offering. He might not be as bad as you think."

"Sure. And pigs might fly past our window at sunset."

She laughs. "What are you going to wear?"

"What do you mean?"

"To the concert tonight."

"I hadn't thought about it."

"You should wear that white dress you bought the other day. It's so cute on you."

"This isn't a date, Josie."

"So? It's a business dinner and a concert. You still need to wear something. And that dress is perfect." She does another Google search and brings up another picture on her laptop. "I can't believe he's the Tucker brothers' cousin. Oh, look, here's a photo of them together. And wow, yeah, you can definitely see the family resemblance." The photo is of Gage, Travis, Vaughn, Kade and two other men. It looks like it was taken several years ago. They're sitting on a dock by a lake. It's summer. They're shirtless and tan and glamorous-looking. "You've got to admit," she says, "there's some killer DNA going on in that family."

"Whatever," I murmur, but I watch as she scrolls further down the search results. "Wonderful," I comment sarcastically. "There he is on his yacht surrounded by supermodels in bikinis. I can hardly wait until he starts banging all our customers."

She clicks on a link to an article and starts reading. "'Gage McCabe might be the most eligible bachelor in Chicago's glitterati dating scene, but good luck pinning him down, ladies. The investment world's golden boy won't commit. He's hot, he's rich, and according to reliable sources, he's a superhero in the sack, with stamina to burn and endowments to die for. But don't expect him to stick around until morning.'"

"'Endowments to die for'?" I grumble. "Eww."

Josie laughs. "Better than being hung like a cocktail weenie. Did you see how he was holding his briefcase? Almost like he was trying to—"

"Would you stop? I don't care how well hung he is! All I care about is putting him on the next plane north."

"Where's your sense of adventure, girl? This will be fun. You get to spend *his* money on *your* dream. You'll finally be able to do it justice."

I continue scrolling, through more photos of Gage McCabe. With an heiress. A Victoria's Secret supermodel. A famous actress. "Looks like he's slept with most of Chicago, L.A., New York and then some. Oh, and here's Nashville."

"No one seems to be complaining." She's still grinning at me. "Maybe it's time for him to conquer Key West."

"Don't. You're a sadist."

She laughs. "I'm an optimist. Oh my God, look at this one. It's a Forbes article written by the CEO of FreshFace Cosmetics, who was formerly a Sports Illustrated swimsuit model: 'I spent six hours in Gage McCabe's company and WOW, it's a six hours I will never, ever forget. Mr. McCabe is beyond gifted and has the one-of-a-kind equipment (*ladies, we're talking *huge*!!*) you want to call all your girlfriends and sing from the rooftops about. He's emotionally distant, yes, but refreshingly up front about it.

He gives you no illusion that he's in this for anything other than smokin' hot sex. And on that front—*fanning myself*—he *more* than delivers (*I'm *still* riding that high*). Damn you, Gage McCabe, for ruining me for anyone else. I'll never forgive you. P.S. call me anytime, sweetie—please!—for another no-strings-attached session. I'm yours xxx.'"

"Jesus. They write articles about it?"

"Let me help you get dressed for tonight."

"No. I'm not wearing that dress. It's way too—"

"Luna. You're going to see the *Tucker Brothers Band* in front row VIP seats with your new hot, rich, well-hung business partner. You'll do as I say. I'm going to blow wave your hair and do your make-up—something under-stated and sexy. And you're wearing that dress. It's my last wish before I set sail for my life of sleep deprivation and diapers. Indulge me and surrender to the process."

Her sassy, caring bossiness happens to be the one thing that's kept me grounded for the past fourteen years. What am I going to do without my best friend? "I'm really going to miss you, Josie."

"I'm going to miss you too, Loon." She gives me a hug and I do my best not to sob my heart out.

If only working sixteen hours a day for years had made more of a difference. If only I'd made enough money to prevent this from happening. If only I wasn't permanently damaged to the point of loathing my new business partner and everything about the way he's conducted his entire life because he's one of *those*, a gorgeous alpha, selected by nature to feel and act in a way that's entitled and thoughtless and self-serving and cruel, just like someone else I knew for a moment in time that I still haven't entirely recovered from. "Hurry up and sign that contract before I change my mind."

"But…are you absolutely sure, honey?"

"Of course I'm sure." I pick up the pen that's sitting on the papers and hand it to her. "Do it."

She scrawls her signature onto the contract.

And that's it. The decision is final. My life has just taken a major turn down an unknowable highway full of smug gauntlets, well-hung corners and arrogant potholes the size of the Grand Canyon.

What have I just gotten myself into?

9

___

GAGE

IT'S NO BIG DEAL, I convince myself. Another woman, another easy seduction. So what if her initial reaction to me—twice—wasn't exactly the idolization I'm used to. Let's not forget who we're talking about here. Me. Gage McCabe, the guy every woman wants and every man wishes they were.

She just needs a little time. Some gentle (or not so gentle) persuasion. By the end of the evening I have no doubt she'll be not only screaming with the kind of pleasure only I can give, but also head over heels.

Why am I even worrying about this? Who's *she*, after all? A debt-ridden waif from Nowheresville, Iowa with a desperate best friend, a floundering business and no safety net.

Why do I care if she falls for me or not?

I don't, is the answer to that question.

Not at all.

But…why was she so goddamn dismissive? Didn't she see *me properly?*

Maybe she needs glasses.

There: *there*'s an imperfection, and it can't be the only one. She'll probably turn out to be a frigid, vacant bitch who'll turn me off as soon as we get into any kind of real conversation. *Every* aspect of her can't be as perfect as the surface appeal.

If she pulls the ice maiden shtick again tonight, then so be it. I'll find someone else. I'll fuck my way through the weekend with a string of women ten times more beautiful than she is. Over the next few weeks I'll turn this business around, exactly the way *I* want to do it. I'll call the shots and who cares if she's on board with them or not? She'll *have* to do what I say, because for all intents and purposes I *own* her and this is going to play out exactly the way *I* want it to.

So there.

Most likely she'll fall helplessly in love with me as I give *her* the cold shoulder, because she deserves a dose of her own medicine. Fuck it. I don't need to plead or beg or buy rinky-dink businesses for the sole reason of getting a woman to go to bed with me.

Once she *does* fall into bed with me, which is inevitable, I'll get her out of my system. Oh, yeah. I'll take my fill—which, if my inferno of a libido has any say in this, might take a fraction longer than my usual wham bam thank you ma'am.

Then I'll return to Chicago and get on with my goddamn life.

It's the *challenge* I'm getting wound up by, that's all this is. Her sassy refusal. Her pixie-cute face with its impertinent little scowl.

I'll wipe that pout right off those bee-stung lips, that's what's going to happen.

Tonight.

I'll lay it on thick as fuck. Because I fucking feel like it.

Women love that shit. They like to feel spoiled and special. *I* can do spoiled and special better than anyone, you bet your ass I can.

I shower and put on jeans, a lightweight shirt and a jacket. I smooth my hair into place and call for a limo. I debate getting flowers but decide it would be over the top. Technically, this isn't a date. It's a business meeting that happens to include some live music.

I'm still not sure why I'm even bothering. And I'm tired of churning about all this. Last night was even worse than the night before. The dreams were even more intense. The lust that's been exploding out of my body is like nothing I've ever experienced. I've morphed into a fucking cum fountain and it's pissing me off to no end because I don't usually have to resort to doing this a cappella. Ever, in fact. Until now.

But I've dealt with that. A lot.

And my cynicism has clicked firmly back into place.

Maybe I won't even go ahead with the ridiculous offer for fifty-one percent of a mediocre business.

What the fuck was I even thinking?

Damn it. The blasé little hell-raiser is really messing with my head. And other parts of me. I've jerked off so much my fucking cock is sore.

It's in this state of mind that I arrive at the Sea Breeze. What kind of name is that, anyway? It's cheesy-sounding. I'll think about changing it and too bad if she doesn't like my decision. I'm pissed off at myself for bothering with all this bullshit in the first place. I could be happily ensconced in a hot tub with two or three naked, willing women by now. I could be licking champagne off their fake tits and not giving a fuck about anything, like I usually do.

It's at that moment that I see her.

She's standing next to the railing of the deck, wearing a fitted sleeveless white dress that hugs her curves and hangs in a flouncy short skirt. Her legs are long and tan. Even from this distance I can see the color of her eyes, a staggered gradient of green, blue and gold. Her cute bob haircut is straighter than it was yesterday, sitting more smoothly and framing her face sort of amazingly. Heart-breakingly. *Ball*-breakingly.

Fucking hell.

It's even worse than the first time. And the second.

I scan the vision of her for flaws. Little details to criticize so I can at least *try* to tone down my reaction.

There are none.

She's fucking perfection, that's all there is to it.

She's talking on the phone, laughing.

A strange urge lodges itself deeply inside my heartbeat.

I really, really want to make her laugh like that.

I have to remind myself to keep breathing. To not halt in my tracks just to stare at her.

Goddamn it.

Why is this happening to me?

I walk closer. Josie's sitting in a chair, watching a jet skier out on the water as Luna talks on the phone.

"I miss you too, Owen," Luna says. "I miss all of you. But I'm not ready to leave Key West. I don't know if I'll ever leave this place. I love it here too much. You should come visit sometime."

I know by now that Owen is Josie's brother. I find myself wondering if *she* loves him like a brother...or something more. Then again, if she loved him like that, wouldn't she want to go back to Iowa with Josie?

Why do I care so much?

"We felt the babies kicking this morning," Luna tells him. "You better take such good care of her." Her easy-going laughter hits me right in the middle of my chest. *Like the hole is still there.* "And tell Marlon he needs to come down here and try out one of these fishing charters. He'd go crazy for the fishing down here."

She notices me then, and her expression takes on an annoyed, provoked edge, like my presence is a dark cloud raining all over her sunny day.

It's true that this isn't the first time I've had people look at me that way, not at all. People I've ruined or fucked and left in the dust.

Usually, I don't care.

Today, I do. A whole fucking lot.

It's a strange feeling. Like I'm losing my grip on something. The total control over everything that I usually bask in feels like it's fraying at the edges, where she's touched it with her golden aura.

WTF?

Maybe I deserve that look. I'm about to take over the controlling share of her beloved business and become the catalyst that sends her best friend back to Iowa. I shouldn't be surprised she's pissed off.

"Listen," she says into the phone. "I have to go. I'll call you once she's on the plane. Yeah, maybe for Christmas. We'll see. All right. Say hi to everyone for me. Bye, Owen. You too." Luna ends the call and hands the phone back to Josie. "Look who's here." She doesn't sound pleased, but I already have my plans in place to thaw out that little iceberg and break down every barrier she's built. *Until she's coming in my mouth as I eat her sweet pussy. Until she's melting around my cock as I fuck her hard and slow.*

Goddamn it.

Jon Lester pitching a no-hitter against Kansas City.

Do. Not. Rise.

Josie watches me approach. I notice then the small stack of papers on the table in front of her. The contract.

"Good evening, ladies," I say. My voice sounds strange. I sound…happy. "How are you tonight?"

"Hi, Gage." Josie, at least, doesn't have laser beams of hatred shooting out of her eyeballs. Probably because I'm about to give her a million dollars.

For half of this run-down old-school Florida bar.

What the hell is wrong with me? Why would I do that?

Because of the way Luna is watching me now, it's as simple as that. I'm paying a million dollars for the opportunity to spend some time with this stunning little tomboy-nymphet, with her crazy eyes and her outrageously stunning face that—for reasons I can't explain at all—makes me feel like I just won some kind of cosmic lottery. It's a face I want to stare at. And kiss. Her body is only highlighting my problem. Especially in that tight little fucking white dress. I can faintly see the beaded tips of her nipples.

I think I'm about to lose my mind. I want to suck champagne off those nipples more than a man crawling across the Sahara in mid-summer wants a glass of water.

And I suddenly understand a lot of things I never understood before.

I'm having some kind of goddamn epiphany.

I can't analyze it right now but I think I might have just realized why my father built a castle for the love of his life. Why my brothers are suddenly acting like they've jumped off the deep end of their sanity.

No.

This isn't me at all.

I don't *want* this overload of amped-up lust. Because it's a lust that has teeth. Teeth that are sinking into the flesh of my soul and spilling venom deep inside me that's tainting me.

With her.

With the memory of how fucking beautiful she is standing here right now in the golden sunlight in her white dress, glaring at me.

"Hi, Luna." I give her the smile that has slayed a thousand women. Okay, not a *thousand*, maybe, but close enough.

Nothing. She doesn't smile back. "Hi, Gage." Feistily. I'm the enemy, clearly, and one she has no time for. *The sex is going to be phenomenal*, is what I'm thinking. At least she called me Gage and not Mr. McCabe, which was starting to sound overdone, like it was bordering on mockery.

Christ, I fucking love the sound of her voice when she says my name. I want to hear her moan it. Scream it. Cry it out in a fit of ecstasy.

"I spoke to Travis a few hours ago," I tell her. "Our

tickets are waiting at the door for us. We're going to have a drink with the boys before their show."

This causes her irritation to lift at the edges. I can detect her excitement.

For *them.* Not me.

I'll fucking kill them!

You won't kill *them, you asshole. They're your goddamn cousins. And you're not a raving psycho. At least you weren't last time you checked.*

Then why do I feel this feverish…insanity? What is it? *Jealousy?*

Yes. I have to win.

I'll change her mind. I'll show her how much she actually wants *me.* I'm better than them. I'm richer. Hotter. Taller, probably. My cock is bigger.

Isn't it?

Yes! Of course it is! It fucking must be. It's ten and a half goddamn inches on a good day. And every day is a good day.

What if you can't change her mind? What if she falls in love with one of them? Or all of them?

Fuck.

Maybe we shouldn't go to the concert tonight. Maybe this was a bad motherfucking idea.

I'm relieved when Josie breaks my ludicrous train of thought. I'm starting to wonder if I really am going crazy. "You guys are going to have *so* much fun," Josie says. "I wish I wasn't exhausted, and also getting on a plane in two days and I still haven't even thought about packing."

"Are you sure you don't want me to stay here and help you?" Luna asks earnestly, like she prefers that option to going out with me.

Is she for real? Are people actually this nice in real life? A small part of me hopes Luna does opt out of our plans tonight. Then I won't have to worry about her fangirling all over my ultra-successful rock star cousins.

I'm even *more* ultra-successful, I remind myself. I have way more money than they do.

"Absolutely not," Josie scolds her. "You're going. You've loved the band since their very first hit. Remember singing along to it that time we drove to Miami? That was such a fun weekend."

Why? Did she meet someone?

Holy hell.

I'm losing it.

I need to calm the fuck down. So I focus on Josie. "Did you read through the contract?"

"Yes. I've accepted your offer and signed it."

My heart actually skips a beat, something I'm not sure it's ever done before. *I get to spend time with her.* I'm going to be Luna's business partner. She'll *have* to hang out with me and do what I tell her to do. "So you agreed to the fifty-one percent?"

"Yes."

My gaze slides to Luna. She's watching me, noticing

the lines of my body. But, still, there's no reaction. No adoration. Not a hint of surrender. Something is holding her back. Despite all this, I can't help grinning at her, even though I'm specifically trying *not* to act like an idiot. Or an asshole. Which isn't easy.

I pull a pen out of my jacket pocket. "May I?" I ask Josie, because to her I'll be polite and gentlemanly. I'll save the beast in me for Luna, once I have her exactly where I want her. All I need to do now is to sign on the dotted line.

Josie slides the papers toward me.

I leaf through the contract to the last page, where I see Josie's scrawled name. Underneath it, I ink my signature.

And that's it. We have a deal.

Before she can change her mind, I take my phone out of my pocket and open up my banking app. I've already set up the transaction. I push the button to transfer one million dollars into Josie's bank account, which I confirmed the details of yesterday. Once it's done, I show Josie the screen.

Transfer of $1,000,000.00 to Josephine R. Farrell complete √

"Wow," she breathes. "Oh my God."

I hold out my hand and Josie takes it. "Thank you," I say, meaning it.

There are more tears in Josie's eyes. "Thank *you,* Gage. This is a dream come true. More than that. It's light years *beyond* the wildest dream I've ever had. And I know you're going to make all Luna's dreams come true too."

You bet your ass I am.

I offer my hand to Luna. The colorful green of her irises has been almost completely swallowed up by the black of her pupils. She fucking hates me. Or maybe there's a part of her that's terrified of me, for some unknowable reason. But she takes my hand anyway because the deal is now done and she's in this, whether she likes it or not.

"I'm looking forward to doing great things together, Luna." *Great, hot, debauched things that make you come hard and scream my name as you dig your fingernails into my back.*

As soon as her cool hand slides into my much larger, hotter one, I feel like I'm having some kind of religious, out-of-body experience. It's the first time she's touched me. Her skin is as soft as silk. There's a current to her touch. An energy. Like she's zapping me with her fierce, electric allure. I can smell the light scent of her tropical, floral-spiced perfume. She's far more beautiful in person even than in my late-night fantasies. I'm so close to her I can count the five golden freckles sprinkled across the bridge of her perfect nose. And there's one near the edge of her plump, full lips. My mouth waters. Her lips are a fraction too full for her face, in the sexiest way imagin-able. They're full and pink with lip gloss. I have a ravenous desire to lick it off, to sink my tongue into her mouth, to devour her and feast on her *until I've come all over her and rubbed myself onto her skin, marking her with my hot cum before holding her down as I fuck her and spend myself deep inside her sweet, nubile little body.* My cock starts to harden and throb and I try desperately to will it not to.

Hellfire and damnation, this is bad.

I hold on to the handshake for too long and she slips her hand from my grasp. "If we don't kill each other first," she says, and it's the first hint of humor aimed in my direction. Maybe because Josie is so happy. Josie stands up, with effort, and gives Luna a hug. They're both crying. For very different reasons.

I give them a minute to let their emotions play out as I slide my phone back into my pocket.

"Go on now," Josie says, wiping her eyes. "You two go and have fun and start making all your grand plans together. I can't wait to see what this place looks like next time I visit with my babies in tow."

"You'll hardly recognize it," I say, and it's true. The only direction is up for this outdated dive, that's for damn sure. And, weirdly, I *do* want to make Luna's dreams come true.

The emotions Luna is empowering are unfamiliar. Usually I do things for other people purely to get something from them. There's always an agenda that leads to *my* satisfaction of one kind or another, most often relating to sex or money or sometimes both.

This feels different. I want to have sex with her—*right now*—but I don't want to *only* have sex with her. I want to please her. And give her things she's never had. I want to inspire more of that bell-chimed laughter.

I don't *want* to want any of these things, but there it is.

"You ready?" I say, more abruptly than maybe I should. I'm agitated. I'm blue-balled and more than half-cocked. I don't like what's happening to me. If I could walk away right now, I would.

Don't be a melodramatic douchebag. Of course you can walk away.

Then do it.

Put some cash in her bank account for the refurbishments, which you can direct from afar, jump on your private jet and get your ass back to Chicago.

No.

I don't want to.

I want to take her out tonight. Then I want to spend the next few days talking through our plans. Watching that outrageous face. Counting those golden freckles. Seeing if I can get her to let me kiss that succulent pink mouth. *And peel off that dress until her full, high breasts bounce free of it so I can taste those little budded nipples and suck on them like the starving wretch that I am.*

I shouldn't be starving, all things considered.

But I am. When it comes to Luna, I suddenly feel like I haven't actually *been* with a woman in years. Maybe ever. Not in a way that actually means something.

Would you fucking listen to yourself?

It's official: I'm going batshit crazy.

"Ready as I'll ever be," she says. Like going out with me is a necessary evil she's dreading.

I'll change all that.

I'm going to show her such a good time she's going to fall in love with me and never want to leave me.

It'll happen. Then I'll lose interest and walk away.

No you won't.

You know it in your twisted, jaded heart that, with this one—*this starry, beautiful girl who's glaring at you and dazzling the hell out of you at the same fucking time*—it was never going to be that easy.

10

I'M NERVOUS ABOUT TONIGHT. I'm having trouble dealing with the avalanche of emotions I'm feeling, that seem to be twisted and entwined in confusing configurations.

There's the fear. Of those long-ago hometown memories—that have suddenly bubbled up in full force after I thought I was done with them, years ago. It's disconcerting. And annoying. There's the sadness, that Josie will be gone by the end of the weekend. It's so sudden and… final. There's the fury, that Gage McCabe has taken total control of my life with one light touch on his fancy iPhone. The smug look on his face when he knew he had me right where he wanted me all along: under his control. I don't *want* to be under his control, or anyone else's, of course I don't. Worst of all are the…*cravings*. The urges I've felt over the past two days that I wish had nothing to do with the unexpected plot twist of the stranger coming to town. That quiet fever in me, like something inside me has just woken up and it's *hungry*. I don't know how to feel about that or what to do about it. And there's excitement. I really do love this band's music.

So, even though Josie insisted on styling me to perfection, I feel out of control under my polished surface layer. The tempest going on in my head and my heart—*and my body*—is making me feel a little crazy.

Gage arrives right on time.

He's dressed in an expensive-looking shirt, a casual jacket and jeans—which I can admit look good. The man definitely knows how to fill out a pair of Levi's. He's tall and athletic-looking. He carries himself like he owns the world.

I guess he sort of does. Or at least a big fat slice of Chicago and now my cute little Key West bar, which happens to be *my* world so, close enough.

"Are you ready?" he asks. His eyes, I notice again, are an unusual shade of blue which could almost be described as a deep, dark teal. The color of a tropical ocean on a stormy day. I don't think I've ever seen eyes that color before.

"Have fun, guys!" Josie waves at us from the doorway, before closing the door to the stairs and waddling her way up. Those twins seem to be growing by the hour. It's good she's going back to Iowa, to her big, loving family and her brand new premium health insurance policy. It makes me feel like the next few hours and in fact the next month will almost be bearable, for that detail alone. Whatever happens, it's worth it. For her, I'll literally do anything. Including jumping off a cliff and straight into ownership by a big city player who could very well be the devil himself.

I stare after her almost wistfully. "Ready as I'll ever be."

Gage's mouth quirks at my reply as he starts walking, hands shoved into his pockets, waiting for me to follow him.

I've decided to make the best of this situation. It's what I do. Besides, this ship has already sailed and I'm now trapped on deck with Captain Cocky.

It's unexpected that I'm suddenly chained so decisively to a loaded player I hardly know, but hell, it could be worse. He could be, I don't know, a shady politician. Or an unethical corporate schmuck. At least when we googled him, a lot of the articles were about how much money he gives to charities. So at least he has *one* redeeming feature…okay, maybe two if you count the unholy fit of those damn jeans. Or the thick dark hair that has a hint of a wave to it. Or the cool alertness in those unusual, tinted eyes that somehow hints at a freakish perceptiveness. Or the absurdly handsome face. Or the impressive width of his shoulders. Or the rugged edge to his clean-cut look…

Okay, so there are a *few* details that could be considered impressive if you were keeping track. Which I'm not.

As I walk alongside him across the deck, I allow myself to briefly fantasize about the improvements we'll be able to make. I'm picturing mood-enhancing lanterns and big-leafed tropical plants. Maybe some white gauzy shade cloths that offer a Caribbean feel. We might even be able to hire extra staff, so some of our workers can have days off once in a while. A weekend here and there, even. I can't remember the last time I had a weekend off.

"It'll be nice to finally get this fixed," I say, running my fingers lightly (so I don't get another splinter) along the rough surface of the railing, where I leaned over it just the other day with my hammer.

"You can tell me all about what you want to do with the place," Gage says. "With no expense spared."

I can't tell if he's just saying that because he knows it's what I want to hear. Or why he would. "Why did you buy this bar?" I ask him, point blank. My fate is already sealed and now I want some answers. "I get that it's cute and has a good vibe and that you saw a business opportunity, but you could have bought your share for a lot less. Why did you offer so much?"

He takes his time, like he's enjoying my anticipation, or whatever this is. "It was undervalued. By a lot. Probably because most buyers don't want the hassle of a fixer upper. It's an absolutely prime location. I know it'll provide a profitable return on investment once it's humming, because we can market it as a destination." It still doesn't add up. "And it was the only way Josie wouldn't have to worry about money for the long term. When I see an opportunity to make someone's day, occasionally I choose to take it."

I find myself glaring at him, which I try to tone down. It's just that…I wasn't expecting him to say that. Or at least say it in a way that seems like he actually means it. "I think you made her millennium."

"Even better."

"I wouldn't have picked you for a guy who likes to make someone else's day."

"Why not?" he asks softly. I wish his ocean-blue eyes didn't feel like they were capable of seeing right into my soul. It's unnerving, like he can read me in ways most people never could or would even want to.

"You seem like you're more interested in making your own day." Oops. I wish I hadn't said that. I'm way too honest sometimes. And I didn't really mean to sound bitchy. So I backtrack and attempt to do some damage control. "I mean…what I meant was that you seem like a guy who looks after his own interests first."

Gage's eyes crinkle at the edges when he smiles. "I guess that's accurate enough."

He opens the gate for me and I walk through it, out onto the sidewalk, where an enormous white limo is parked in front of the restaurant.

"What jerk parked a limo here? It's blocking the entire entrance."

"Um…this one." His smile lingers.

"Oh. This is yours?"

"It's ours. To take us to the gig."

Wow. I'm so used to scrimping and saving, the extravagance of it seems wildly unnecessary. "We don't need a limo. Think of all the gas this thing will guzzle. Not to mention the impact on the environment."

"We're driving two miles, if that. The environment will be fine."

I'll admit I'm overreacting slightly. But he's *so* high-handed. I feel the perverse desire to cut him down a notch, so I can at least be on even ground. "It's exactly that kind of attitude that's caused irreversible damage to the environment in the first place. No one ever thinks it's them personally, but it's the accumulation of seven billion carbon footprints—"

"I gave two million dollars last month to a bio-fuel company that's offsetting the effects of my own personal carbon footprint plus those of around four million other people, for exactly that reason: so I can take a limo when the occasion calls for one."

He did? I guess that's sort of impressive. Still, it's wasteful. "But we can walk to Duval Street from here. It only takes ten minutes."

"The show's not on Duval Street. It's at a secret venue. And I was going to offer you a glass of champagne on the way." He pauses before he says it. "You seem like you could use one."

"What's that supposed to mean?"

"You seem a little…wound up."

I realize my fists are actually balled and resting on my hips in a sort of pissed-off stance. It's *him*. He has an absolute knack for ruffling me! And the crazy edge to my emotions is having its way with me again. "I guess I am just the tiniest bit 'wound up', now that you mention it, yes." I say it using air quotes, sort of bitchily, yes—because he deserves it! First he thinks he's God's gift, then he forces through his ownership of my bar and now he's *insulting* me? That's just great. "Let's see if I can think of why I might be *wound up*. Hmm, maybe because my best friend is about to go through the hardest thing that's ever happened to her and I won't be there for her, like we've been there for each other every day, through everything— which at times has been a lot—for the past fourteen years. It *means* something to me that I won't be there to make sure she's okay. Maybe you don't get that. And even though her family is awesome and they'll do the best they can, it doesn't change the fact that she's alone in the most profound way it's possible to even *be* alone because the father of her babies was never in the picture and never will be. And some days that's going to be really, really hard for her." Not that Gage would ever understand loyalty. "And, oh yeah, let's not forget the part about how I'm now professionally and financially chained to a perfect stranger who's in total control of my money, my business—which is the only thing in the world that's ever felt like mine, but no longer does—and basically my entire life. So please forgive me if I seem *wound up*." He's absolutely right, I *am* wound up. Very. I don't even care that I'm ranting.

Gage is staring down at me from his six feet and possibly three or four inches and there's something in his expression that could almost be mistaken for empathy. I'm five-six on a good day so the height differential is noticeable. He's big and sexy as hell and sort of intimidating, even though I'm not a person who gets intimidated easily. *Why does he have to be so damn beautiful?* It's only making this whole thing harder. "What happened to the guy?" His voice is low and has a husk to it that has no doubt caused legions of supermodels to drop their panties on the spot. He doesn't rise to my rant. At all. Of course he doesn't. He probably deals with ranting women every day of the week. Because he's a philandering, self-important prick, that's why.

"What guy?"

"The father of Josie's babies."

"Oh. He— " I pause because…should I tell him the truth? Then I remember that he knew the exact value of our freaking *chattels* so he could probably find out anything he wants to know. It doesn't really matter now anyway. "It was a one-night stand. She never found out his last name and by the time she discovered she was pregnant he was gone and we couldn't find him. All we knew was that his name was Noah and he was from California."

"Do you think she'd want to find out who he is?"

"Of course she would. She was devastated that we couldn't find any trace of him. If nothing else, she just wanted to tell him. She said he was a really nice person. He seemed kind, she said."

His eyes narrow like he's making a mental note of something. He opens one of the rear passenger doors of the limo. "You can still be there for Josie as much as you need to be. Our budget includes upgrades to all the latest devices as well as travel accounts and the use of my private jet. You can visit her whenever you want. Put her on video conference 24/7 if that makes this easier. We'll fly her to Key West after the babies are born and you can be there for her every step of the way. It's not hard to communicate hourly these days, if that's what you want to do. As for the part about the perfect stranger... 'perfect' might be mildly overstating it, but close enough."

I'm sort of reeling from all the things he just said. It takes me a second to realize...is that a joke?

Gage laughs, so I guess it is. "Get in," he says.

"No." I'm still pissed off for ten different reasons. Top of the list is that my fury is so damn entertaining to him.

"I'll double my investment in bio-fuel next month so I can offset *both* our carbon footprints if it makes you feel better. A glass of champagne might take your mind off the ecosystems for an hour or two, let's try it."

Let's try it? He really is a high and mighty piece of

work. "I don't want to try it. And I don't drink champagne."

"Why not?"

"It's…expensive." *Shit. Why did I admit that?*

Another smile. "I'm buying. Come on, we have something to celebrate. And when I celebrate I do it properly."

At this point I feel like arguing with him just for the hell of it. *How does he get under my skin so easily?* I have an uncontrollable desire to rile him, like he's doing to me. I exhale a cynical laugh. "Please."

"Please what?"

"Please spare me your sanctimonious M.O. Your way of doing things *properly* has basically destroyed my life. What looked like paradise just a few short days ago now looks more like a steaming pile of…rubble."

"I haven't destroyed it. I've enhanced it." His ego might as well be Mount Everest.

"Of course. Now that you're in it, my life is suddenly overflowing with unicorns and butterflies."

At this he laughs. *Goddamn him, he's gorgeous.* "I can arrange butterflies. Unicorns is a big ask, but I'll see what I can do."

Jerk! He *loves* that he's winding me up. He's rolling around in my rage like a pig in springtime mud, enjoying every minute of it.

I take a deep breath, willing myself to calm down. For two years I've meditated and practiced yoga every morning, so I'm usually pretty good at steadying my nerves when I need to. But right now it hardly helps. "Listen—" I almost call him Mr. McCabe again but then I remember we're on a first name basis now that he owns me. "Gage. There's no need to ply me with champagne. You've already won."

"I didn't realize this was a competition."

"I think we both know that's not true." *And* that he's already crossed twelve finish lines before I've even started the race.

"And I wasn't intending to 'ply' you with anything."

This whole thing was obviously a terrible idea. We don't have anything in common and can't agree on a single thing. Not even the Tucker Brothers Band is worth putting up with *this* for an entire evening. "You know what, I think maybe I've changed my mi—"

His phone rings loudly, interrupting me in mid-excuse.

Gage pulls his phone out of his pocket. The screen says *Travis*. "Do you mind if I take this? It's probably about our tickets."

I shrug insolently. He can take whatever call he wants.

He puts his phone on speaker. "Travis."

"Gage. Where are you, man?"

"On my way now."

"Come around to the back. There's been another leak about the gig tonight. There's already a crowd at the front door. We're still going ahead but we're hoping it doesn't get too crazy."

"Shit."

"Yeah. How long 'til you get here?"

"Around ten minutes, depending on traffic."

Wow. That's Travis Tucker. A real live rock star. Last night I listened to a few of their new songs as I was falling asleep. They're *amazing*. All three of the brothers write songs and each of their styles is slightly different. Travis's skew more country, Vaughn's are more rock 'n roll and Kade's are, if I had to try to describe them, dreamier. More poetic and soulful. The band has evolved over the past two years to write songs that go beyond stadium anthems into something far more original. It would be a shame to miss a show like this one, especially since I'll get a chance to actually *meet* them.

I'm sure I'll regret it if I bail now.

Still talking to Travis as he holds the limo door open, Gage flicks his eyebrows in a *let's go* gesture.

Oh, what the hell. I do it. I slide into the limo to the far side of the seat. Gage slides in next to me and shuts the door. The driver starts the car and we start heading toward Old Town.

"We'll have a cold one ready for you," Travis is saying.

"Make it two," Gage tells him. "I'm bringing someone."

"Oh, right. The same one you came to Key West to visit?"

Gage's mouth quirks almost guiltily and there's a

mischievous spangle in his blue eyes as he looks up at me. "No."

Of course. Travis is probably referring to the woman who threw the drink in Gage's face that first night he came into the bar with his shirt still wet. Which only cements the fact that Lothario over here is what he is: a serial womanizer. I could see that about him from the very first second I met him.

"See you soon," he says to Travis. Then he ends the call.

Gage takes the bottle of champagne that's chilling on ice and pours a glass. He hands it to me. Despite my earlier tirade, I take it. Maybe it *will* help me relax a little.

He fills his own flute, then he clinks his glass against mine. As he watches me take a sip of the bubbling liquid, I can detect a playful, intense ember behind his blue gaze, like there are things going on inside his head that I really wish…weren't. This is what he does, after all. Every night of the week most likely. "Please don't get any ideas." *Shit. Why did I say it like that?*

"What kind of ideas were you expecting me to get?" Smooth as velvet.

"I just want to make sure we're on the same page. About this being strictly a business meeting."

"Of course. We'll talk about the ozone layer and listen to some music and celebrate the exciting potential of our business, that's what we're here for." His eyelashes are dark and dense, a fraction too long for a such a masculine hunk of a man. It's like that with him. I've never met a more manly-looking man in my life but there are also details of him that could only be described as beautiful. The way his dark eyelashes sweep sort of poetically. The changing color of his eyes, like a mood ring. The way his thick hair frames his head gracefully. His rugged style. He sure did win the good looks lottery.

And he clearly uses it to his advantage, which makes me feel like I'm standing on shaky ground. Meanwhile *he* couldn't appear to be any more relaxed if he tried.

It makes me wonder if anything ever gets to him. If he has moments of weakness.

I guess when you're as hot and rich and successful as he is you don't have to worry about weaknesses.

"To success." He spins the word to sound…dirty, as though his definition of success has more than one meaning. He raises his glass and gives me a slow, scorching look that basically fries every brain cell I possess.

Damn it.

I need my brain cells to *work* right now, and be firing on all their goddamn cylinders. I need every shred of self-possession I can wrangle. Because Gage McCabe is not only fiendishly smart, he's also a man who could easily reduce me to a thoroughly-female mess of desire, I'm learning. My forcefield is cranked up as high as it'll go, because he's doing that alpha thing again. Emitting top shelf pheromones that no doubt slay debutants by the dozens. It's his superpower, this is obvious. He's using those turquoise eyes to hypnotize me and that big, male body to lure me in.

If I hadn't been through the ringer once already, I might fall for it. I might accept his challenge and let him do the things I can absolutely tell are playing out in his filthy mind. His eyes wander down my body, lingering. *He's picturing me naked. Wet. Ready. He's thinking about what he'd do with his mouth.*

Help me.

The truth is, though, I *have* been burned. Badly. And I honestly can't go there again. Especially without Josie.

So I crank up my forcefield one notch higher and I do the things I do best. Deflect and avoid. Look on the bright side. Pretend everything's fine. Smooth things over with cheerful conversation. Make small talk with every Joe who walks into my bar so they feel comfortable there.

I say the first thing that pops into my mind, because breaking this intense silence and distracting him toward safer directions is the only shield I have. "The last time I was in a limo I was nine years old. I used to have to ride in one to get to school every day."

"In New York?"

There's something jarring about his question. "How did you know that?"

For a split second, I get the feeling he might be hiding

something, but he glides past it. "I don't. It was just a guess. There are a lot of limos there."

"Good guess." Maybe he googled me. No, he definitely would have googled me. I already know he's thorough. And it isn't that hard to find out about where people have lived these days. So I brush it off. "It was one of the perks, if you could call it that, of having a loaded real estate mogul lusting after my beautiful, desperate mother, who was more than willing to take every gift he was dumb and eager enough to give."

"You didn't like the guy?" His hands are tanned and strong-looking. He could break the stem of that champagne flute without even trying. His jacket is unbuttoned. His blue shirt, made of expensive cotton, is stretched across his broad chest. His belt is thick, well-worn leather, almost cowboy-ish. Under it, his stomach is washboard flat. In fact there's not a hint of anything other than pure, hard muscle anywhere on him. His thighs, lovingly hugged by his faded jeans, are strong and athletic-looking. I can abstractly appreciate that he's perfectly built. And my eyes, since they happen to be checking out the general area, can't help but skim...*the incredibly...huge, bold shape of his—*

Sweet Jesus.

I concentrate instead on the beads of condensation dripping down the bottle of Moët. *Anything but his "endowments to die for." They really weren't kidding.* Somehow, I regain my composure. "I…I didn't hold it against him. It wasn't his fault he was being played."

"Maybe he didn't mind," he purrs. "Maybe it was worth it to him."

As our eyes meet, something passes between us. Some kind of unspoken comeback. *Like you would be*, he seems to be saying.

I feel the heat rise to my cheeks. Good Lord, what corner of my jaded mind did *that* morsel of self-flattery crawl out of? The champagne must be messing with my head. Not that I *don't* think I'd be worth it—I would. I'm a self-sufficient, level-headed, fun-loving girl who's a little on the scrawny side, whose hair is a little less controllable than I'd like it to be and whose bank balance leaves a lot to be desired, but other than that I'm happy enough with my looks, my morality and the space in the universe I occupy the best I can. I'm a good friend and a nice person. But the thought of Gage McCabe finding me *worthy* of anything at all is crazy and also would never in a million years happen.

Because I won't let it.

I can't.

I wouldn't survive it twice.

"Well, even if it *was* worth it to him, it wore off," I tell him.

"What happened?"

I'm not sure why he'd be hanging on every word of my story, but he seems genuinely interested. "My mother found out he was cheating on her with four of the women in her book club, so she divorced him and accepted the marriage proposal of the COO of Quaker Oats. I think she married him mainly for his country club membership. So we moved to Iowa. It was a big change from New York but at least her new husband was faithful and, more importantly, rich. Not quite in Husband Number Two's league but she could drink gin and play bridge and sit by the pool all day, which worked just fine for her."

I wish I wasn't telling him this stuff, but I need to do something to fill the heavy-in-ways-I-can-barely-but-am-determined-to-handle silence.

"What about now? Is she still there?" I get that strange vibe again that he already knows the answer to his own question.

"No. Husband Number Four has a bungalow in the Hollywood Hills once owned by one of the Gabor sisters. My mother even started smoking her cigarettes through one of those hand-held plastic filters. But after a major sex scandal involving several of her husband's top producers—and him—his movie studio has been hemorrhaging money. So I'm sure my mother is currently in the process of scouting around for her next sugar daddy." It doesn't exactly bring back heart-warming family memories. "What about you? Have you always lived in Chicago?"

"I grew up in Ann Arbor. I moved to Chicago after college to get my MBA and start my third company."

Third? So he has bought and sold a few of them. "What number is my bar? Out of all the businesses you've built or bought?"

His smile is lazy but alert. Dazzling, you could say. If you were susceptible to things like that. "A lot. Too many to count."

"Try. I'm curious."

He thinks about it for a second. "Maybe forty, give or take."

Wow. No wonder it all feels less than personal to him. "How old are you?"

He laughs at my directness. "How old do you think I am?"

I already know, from one of Josie's online searches. "Twenty-seven."

Still smiling. "Good guess."

"You're not going to ask how old I am?"

He's unrepentant. "It made sense for me to do my research. It's what I tend to do before I invest my money. I happen to know you turned twenty-three two weeks ago."

"I suppose you know my birth date, star sign and favorite color too."

"November 7th. Which I guess would make you a Scorpio, I think it is. And, if I had to guess, I'd say your favorite color is…yellow." He gets an almost dreamy look as he says the word.

I watch his face, more fascinated than I'd like to

admit. It's not the kind of thing you can google. "You're right."

This time his smugness is laced with a subdued but genuine delight. And it *hurts*, weirdly. Somewhere behind my rib cage. He's just so outrageously stunning.

There's an almost stricken edge to my voice. "What else did you find out?"

"Just what I came across as I was looking into the business records. Your birth date happened to be listed on the company details."

It makes me wonder if he knows anything about…the monster under my bed. But how could he? Secrets like that aren't listed on Google. So I steer the conversation back toward him. "Is your family still in Ann Arbor?"

"My two brothers are. My parents checked out around five years ago."

"I'm sorry."

It's a weird way to put it. *Checked out.* And he seems uneasy with the subject. But then he says, "They were very much in love, right up until they died."

I smile at him, sort of sadly. What a concept. "I've never met anyone in love."

"Really?" Like this is shocking to him.

"No."

He blinks at me. There's a softness to his manner when he's thinking about his family that clashes with the killer playboy side of him. "That's too bad. Although I used to think love was overrated."

I'm almost afraid to ask it. "Used to?"

He smiles, and for a split second his intensity reaches a place inside me most things don't. A hidden place that's not so much forgotten as never even discovered. "Yeah."

But then I remember the woman he came to Key West to see. The models and the heiresses and the girls in the article who raved about his endowments then cried because he's never there by morning. So I keep it light. "What do your brothers do in Ann Arbor?"

"Bo is still in college, studying business, playing quarterback. Like Caleb did before he joined up and deployed. And like I did." This information hits me hard, right in the middle of my gut. *He's a quarterback. Of course he is.* "Caleb just got back from a year in Afghanistan."

"Oh. I'm…" My heart is beating fast. I take a drink of my champagne and end up drinking half the glass.

Gage notices. "You okay?" He puts a big, warm palm on my bare arm, as though to calm me.

I try not to jerk away from him. I ease back until he's no longer touching me. "I'm fine." *Except that he was a quarterback too. A quarterback who made sure I now have an unreasonable aversion to football, hometowns and, come to think of it, men in general.* "Just, um…really thirsty."

It was a long time ago, Luna. You really need to get over it.

Maybe I can't. Maybe I'm just…broken.

I wait for my heartbeat to slow as he tops up my glass again. "There's plenty more where that came from."

I don't want more champagne. I want to go back to

my apartment. I want to vent to Josie. I want her to give back the money and cancel this whole thing.

But the limo pulls to a stop and I can see out the tinted windows that we're in a back alley.

The driver is already opening the door for us.

"We're here," Gage says.

INSIDE, there's already a crowd. It's a large, funky venue with low ceilings and distressed wood that's been decorated with license plates, maps, photos and retro Americana knickknacks. A long bar runs the full length of the left side of the room, where some of the barstools are already occupied. Around thirty square tables are crammed into the space, each with a little red lamp on it, and there's a raised wooden stage in one corner. Roadies are tinkering with the sound system and beefy security guards are manning the front door. Outside its small, barred window I can see the crowd gathering.

"Where's the band?" Gage asks one of the roadies, and the guy points to a doorway.

Gage stays close to me, in a way that could almost be…protective. He's not as relaxed as he was before, not at all. He hasn't touched me again since my mini-meltdown in the limo but he's watching me. It makes me wonder if he *gets* things, like he has a radar for understanding that people come with baggage. Maybe because his brother is a soldier. Or because his parents "checked out." There's a story there I wouldn't dream of asking about, but I could tell the whole topic was something that weighs heavily, not surprisingly.

We walk into another room, crowded with people and loud music, where there's a pool table. I recognize them even before they see Gage.

It's the Tucker Brothers Band.

Wow.

It's crazy to walk into a room and see people whose music you've been listening to religiously for almost two years, standing here, playing pool. I listen to their music most nights as I'm falling asleep. Their melodies are inked into my brain at this point. Their songs dig deep and there have been many times when I've used their words to feel better and to lift myself up. Everyone gets the blues sometimes. Everyone feels things harder some days than others. Their music reminds me of that.

They're even more good-looking in person than they are in their videos. Hot and edgy in a wholesome but rocket-fueled kind of way. Country boys with a rock and roll vibe.

But it's a funny realization: Gage, as they man-hug him and pat him on the back, seems somehow even *more* technicolored. Larger than life and more in sync with my own emotions. Maybe because I've spent time with him. Or because I've detected things under his surface level that have affected me more deeply than I was expecting.

Don't even think about it, girl. For you he spells heartbreak on steroids.

"Luna," Gage says, gently grasping my arm with his warm hand again. This time, I allow it. "These are my cousins, Travis, Vaughn and Kade. Luna is my new business partner." Gage is standing so close to me, if we were in a less crowded space I'd have the urge to step back. As it is, there's something almost comforting about the way he's so big and shielding, in this crowded room full of people.

All three of them check out Gage's "date"—*me*, not that I *am* his date, of course—with fascination. Like he's never introduced someone to his cousins before.

Travis Tucker looks like he just stepped out of a wheat field. His hair is sun-lightened, his skin is tanned and his flannel shirt is worn in. His eyes are bright green. He's got a laid-back, friendly smile that makes you wish *you* were from Nashville, because it must be a good place if it could produce a man like him, a down-home country boy with a talent-infused X-factor and good looks to write home about. Vaughn has black hair, bronzed skin, a lot of ink on his muscular arms and bright blue eyes. For all his colorfulness, he's got a rough-edged recklessness to him that fits his reputation to a T. He's the wild child of the group, the one who's often in the headlines for his loose behavior, his stints in rehab and his genius on the drums. Kade has a different vibe altogether. His hair is longer than his brothers, also sun-bleached, and his eyes are just as blue, but at first impression he's deeper and not as outgoing as the other two. I heard him described once as a "dreamy bad boy," and the description fits. He's soulful, even on the surface, and I happen to know that his songs are some of the most beautifully-written of any I've heard. It's *his* lyrics that I've memorized most of all to find strength on those nights when I needed a little extra.

"I love your music," I tell them honestly.

Travis smiles. I can see the family resemblance. He looks like Gage, in the shape of his eyes and the raw sex appeal. Josie was right, there's some seriously killer DNA going on in this family.

"So glad you could make it tonight, Luna," Travis says.

"Hey there, Luna," Kade drawls, then he glances at Gage, like there's something uncharacteristic about the way Gage is behaving. In fact all three of them are watching the way he's still holding my arm and standing over me like an over-zealous bodyguard, eyeballing them as though he might lunge at one of them any minute.

Vaughn laughs and pats Gage on the back. "Okay, bro, we get it."

Get what?

"Business partners, huh." Travis winks at me.

Vaughn elbows Gage playfully before reaching out to

take my hand. "Nice to meet you, Luna." He kisses my knuckles in an old-fashioned, gentlemanly way. Either he's being mischievous or his mother hammered home some manners, I can't quite figure out which. "Well done, taming this one. We never thought we'd see the day."

Tamed?

Gage watches the exchange like a hawk, then he removes my hand from Vaughn's and good-naturedly—almost—steers Vaughn toward the pool table.

"Don't even think about it," Gage tells him casually, but there's something feral about the blue glint in his eyes.

Vaughn laughs. "No need to go caveman."

I give Gage a look. *What the hell is he doing? Staking some kind of claim on me?* I don't want him to do that, not that I'm interested in any of the Tucker brothers, who all have women swarming around them like bees to honey, hanging off their every word. But we agreed this would be strictly business and that's the way I intend to keep it. Eventually, when I decide I'm ready to dive back into the shark-infested waters of the dating scene, it sure as hell won't be with someone who's banged so many women they write articles in freaking Forbes about it. *No matter how hot he is or how restless I might be feeling tonight.*

He grins down at me, his eyes blazing with volatile energy.

Vaughn waves down a waitress. "Bring us a round of JD shots. We'll take five."

A petite woman with dark hair, jean shorts, long legs,

cowboy boots and the energy of a firecracker launches herself at Gage and gives him a huge hug. "My favorite cousin's in town and no one even *told* me?" she squeals.

Gage kisses her on the cheek. "Last time you saw Bo you said the same thing to him, and the time before that you said it to Caleb."

"Well, tonight *you're* my favorite cousin. It's been way too long."

Gage sets her down. She notices me and the way Gage is standing so close to me, and she gives me a curious once-over. Gage makes the introductions. "Roxie, this is Luna LaRoux, my brand new business partner. Luna, my cousin Roxie. She's the youngest in the family and the manager of the band."

"Nice to meet you, Luna."

"You too, Roxie."

"What kind of business are you in?" she asks. By this point we sort of have to shout to hear each other. The place is filling up.

"I own a bar, not too far from here," I tell her.

I would guess that Roxie is around my age. She's gorgeous, with the same dark hair as Gage and Vaughn, and violet irises. She blinks long eyelashes at Gage and shakes her head. "Since when are you in the hospitality business, cousin? Wait, let me guess. As soon as you laid eyes on this one." She laughs and I'm about to explain—again—that she's got the wrong idea. "She seems way too nice for you, Gage."

"I'm nice," Gage says, as a wolfish smile lurks at the corner of his mouth. "Most of the time."

The waitress arrives and places five shots on the edge of the pool table.

Roxie puts her hands on her hips. "Vaughn Tucker, I told you no more shots."

Vaughn smiles at her impishly and runs a hand through his disheveled hair, messing up the shiny mop of it even more. "We always have three before a show, you know that, Rox, and so far we've only had one. Otherwise we don't play as well. Three is our lucky number."

"Lucky number, my ass," Roxie says. "I said we're changing that rule."

"Just because you don't drink doesn't mean we can't." Their companionable bickering makes it clear they enjoy each other's company. It's easy to see that Vaughn is a guy who pushes every boundary. And that he can get away with it nine times out of ten. He laughs, handing a shot to Gage and one to me.

I'm about to refuse the shot, but how often do I get a dose of the Tucker brothers' good luck? Besides, I'm more of a Jack Daniels girl than a champagne enthusiast.

Vaughn passes shots to his two brothers and all four of the men tip them back.

I drink mine and it burns all the way down.

"You guys are on stage in five," Roxie tells the band. "We have to start earlier than planned because it's all over

Twitter that we're playing here tonight and security is getting nervous. We might have to bail early."

"Shit," says Vaughn. To the waitress: "One more round, then."

It's probably not a good idea, especially after two glasses of champagne, but I go with it anyway. I hardly ever drink or go out or do anything besides work so why not live a little, I figure.

We follow Roxie into the main room where the band takes to the stage. Gage leads me through the crowd to the best table in the house, to the left of the stage. There's a reserved sign on the table. Gage and I take our seats as the lights dim. The place is completely packed. There's a line of security guards barricading the door. It makes me wonder how many people are waiting outside, trying to get in.

"Thanks for comin' tonight," drawls Travis. He strums a familiar chord. "You know we love playing to smaller crowds like this because they remind us of where we came from. They remind us about what's important in life, like close friends and a good laugh. Like a Nashville sunset. We're going to sing a song for you now about exactly that. It's called Tennessee Sundown."

The crowd cheers.

I *love* this song. It's one of their old ones, from their first album.

As they start playing and I listen to the words I know by heart, I feel that pang I sometimes do, the one that comes along with having a broken family, a pieced-together life of my father's and stepfathers' infidelities and my mother's quiet desperation. A life that never included a sense of belonging to something bigger than myself and my own grit. That's why Josie's family felt like a refuge to me. But even with all the dinners around their big dining room table and the summer afternoons by the swimming hole, it still wasn't *my* family. Not really. I belonged but I wasn't one of them. I didn't look like a Farrell or act like a Farrell or have the same history or the same stories. Because I wasn't one of them. I was me, all along. My own entity of one.

What a gift it must be to grow up like these siblings. Linked to your own band of laughter and memories and belonging and love.

And it makes me think about what Gage said, about his parents. *They were very much in love, right up until they died.*

It must be a beautiful thing, to love like that. To know that there's at least one person on this Earth who's got your back, who'll be there for you every step of the way, who will love you just because you're *you*. Someone to share a life with and build your own close-knit family with, day by day. It's hard to imagine. A best friend is one thing but true love really must be the ultimate lucky score.

I happen to glance over at Gage at that exact moment. The look on his face is…something I might never forget. It's layered and contemplative. He's been watching me. The soft shadowed light flatters him, like every light does. There's none of the playboy in him at this exact moment. There's heat and that purely-masculine swagger, but also a tenderness that catches me off guard. He overcomes it, like I've busted him, and the aloof charisma clicks back into place. He stands up and holds out his hand. "Dance with me."

Of course he issues it as a command rather than a question, but whatever. I do want to dance. The dance floor in front of the stage is already packed. The music sounds ten times better live. You can *feel* the emotion thrumming out of every husky word and every vibrating note. The strum of Kade's bass guitar hits you somewhere deep inside the broken pieces of your own goddamn soul.

Okay, maybe that whiskey is starting to have its way with me.

But I take Gage's hand—which feels warm and strong enough to secure my balance—and he leads me down to the crowded dance floor. He's tall, and *big*. I've never thought of myself as tiny or fragile, but in his grasp I can feel his energy and his brimming strength. Maybe it's the whiskey or the champagne or the music or some combination of all three, but the thought of him overpowering me—which he could obviously very easily do—doesn't feel threatening to me, not tonight. It feels sort of…*hot.*

I'm mortified to realize that my nipples are beading into tight buds. And my panties feel damp, clinging to me intimately…*there,* where a warm pulse plays. *Oh God.*

To most women this wouldn't be a big deal. To me, it is. It's been a long time since I've been this close to a man. It was an experience that changed me. It shut me down and basically broke me. And I've been avoiding anything like *this* ever since.

Which, of course, sucks.

Tonight, the whiskey is helping. And so does the fact that a certain big city playboy is a seriously good dancer. He holds me against his ludicrously hard body and leans down to my ear so I can hear him above the noise. "What were you thinking about just then?"

It sort of amuses me that I have this small power over him. He owns my bar, he has more money than God and he weighs as much as three of me. But he can't read my mind. And it's bugging him that he doesn't know.

"I was thinking about how I don't appreciate you going 'caveman' when we agreed this was a business meeting."

He shakes his head, more relaxed now. "Trust me, that wasn't caveman. That was a flea on a mammoth the caveman was about to hunt down with his bloody, razor-sharp spear."

I laugh, confused. "What?"

Gage wraps his arm around me more tightly and sways to the song. He's so strong I have no choice but to sway along with him. He holds me close against the outrageous planes of his big body.

God.

Is he…*hard?*

Holy hell, he is. And he's huge…if that's what that even is.

It must be, unless he's carrying a wooden club in his pocket.

Good Lord.

I try to create a distance between us but he's far too strong, holding far too tightly. I can see he's making an effort to control himself, but it doesn't seem to be working. He's hot to the touch and practically vibrating with fizzing intensity. "I was just looking out for you. I can't have my cousins harassing my new business partner. They can't be trusted."

"Well, thanks, but I can look out for myself."

"I'm afraid that's part of the contract. It's in my own best interests to make sure you're happy and well-adjusted at all times."

"Well-adjusted? You're a little late for that. That ship sailed years ago."

His smile is almost sympathetic. "You and me both. I'll settle for happy, then."

My laugh is slightly scoffing. "You think *you* can make me happy?"

That jungle-cat arrogance. "Yes."

I'm aware of the hard ridges of his body—and one extremely *huge* ridge in particular. *Endowments to die for indeed.* "How?"

My body, against my will, is reacting to his heat and his outrageous hardness. My breasts are pressed against his big, broad chest and my nipples feel taut and hyper-sensitive. A fresh warmth dampens my panties even more. *God. This is bad.* "I'd start by asking you what you hope for. What your wildest dreams are. What hurts and what makes you cry. What your favorite songs are and which movies you watch over and over. I'd take you to the places you've always wanted to go. I'd find out what makes you laugh. And then I'd do everything I could to kill off the painful things and at the same time I'd shower you with the good stuff, so much so that you couldn't help but be happy."

I stare up at him as we gently sway to a slow song. It might be the nicest thing anyone has ever said to me. I fight off the sting of tears behind my eyes. Because no one, aside from maybe Josie, who already knows every-thing about me, has ever asked those kinds of questions, or cared enough to find out.

But then I remember who I'm dealing with here. *Gage McCabe is the most eligible bachelor in Chicago's glitterati dating scene, but good luck pinning him down, ladies.*

I feel a pang of sadness, that he is what he is…and that I am what I am. It's too bad, because the sparking heat in the charged contact between us is just about the best feeling I've had in…*okay, maybe ever.* "I bet you say that to all the girls," I say dismissively.

"As a matter of fact, I've never said it to anyone."

"Then why are you saying it to me?"

"Because." Our gazes lock but, with effort, I break the

trance. *Careful, Luna,* I remind myself. The scars of my past burn hotly somewhere behind my soul.

"'Because' isn't an answer."

"Tell me what you were really thinking about, before. I don't think it was cavemen."

The whiskey is starting to hit my system, like a warm, loosening current. "I was thinking about love and what it might feel like," I tell him honestly. "Have you ever been in love, Gage?"

"No."

"Really? Not even once?"

"Not even a little."

"I should've expected that from you, I guess." He's like a junkyard dog who's only out for one thing.

"Why do you say that?"

"With all your experience and to never even connect with someone like that…do you ever wonder if you're even capable of love?" *Why am I even bringing this up?* Maybe because I'm wondering if *I* am, considering my upbringing and my past. Maybe some people just aren't wired that way, for whatever reasons.

His eyes are a brilliant blue even in the low light, like pressed sea glass with moonlight shining through. "Yes. I used to wonder about that all the time."

There it is again. *Used to.* Before I can ask him what he means, someone screams.

Very suddenly, the whole room erupts. The back door

has been breached, and the bar floods with loud, drunk, raucous people.

The band is quickly surrounded by security and ushered off stage, through a door I hadn't noticed before. They have to fight people off. The fans are screaming and crying, swarming in a thick pack, trying to get closer to the Tucker brothers. It's like a riot. People are crazy and out of control, pushing and yelling.

My God. This is dangerous. It's a stampede.

Gage picks me up and pushes us through the crowd. People swear at us as Gage's big, wide-shouldered form shelters me and breaks through the throngs. He does this far more easily—almost tactically—than most people might have. He's a quarterback, I remember. No wonder. But the crowd gets thicker. More people are screaming. And we're not any closer to the exit.

Gage finds a door and shoves us through it, slamming it behind us.

It's dark in here. And the noise outside is suddenly muffled and quiet. It's a tiny space, and narrow. The crack of light from around the door allows enough light in to see that it's an equipment closet. There are a few microphone stands and some wound-up cords hanging from hooks. There's an old-fashioned key in the door, which Gage turns, locking us in.

"I hope we don't get stuck in here," I whisper.

"We won't. Are you all right, honey?"

"I think so. Do you think the band is okay?"

"They'll be fine. They have plenty of security."

My heart is racing.

Gage's is too. I can feel it. He's still holding me and he leans me against the wall. But he doesn't back away. He's pressed up hard against me, like his protective instincts won't let him distance himself. His large, warm hand rests against my face, as though he's feeling me for signs of distress or injury. The back of his knuckles graze my cheek. "Are you sure you're okay?"

I'm breathing hard. "Yeah. Are you?"

He doesn't answer. His chest rises and falls with his heavy breath. The scent of him, of leather and man-spiced adrenaline and a hint of whiskey, is…dizzying… intoxicating. Here, in this dark space like a calm, intimate haven inside the eye of a raging hurricane, I feel safe. From them.

Not from him.

Not from myself and the addictive, rushing urges coursing through my body.

He smells so good.

He feels so good.

Much, much too good.

He smooths a stray strand of my hair back, tucking it behind my ear with strong fingers. Despite the gentle gesture, his eyes are bright with lust.

Gage leans closer.

I place two fingers against his lips, to stop him.

If I kiss him, or give him any piece of myself…I don't

want him to be gone by morning. I can't be casual. I care. I *feel*, too much.

"I want to taste you, sweet girl, so much. I've been dreaming of—"

"No," I whisper. *Oh God.* The way we're positioned, with my knees apart and his big body not allowing me to close them. The enormous bulk inside his jeans is *right there*—pressed hard against the thin layer of my hitched-up skirt and the thin silk of my saturated panties. These delicate barriers aren't enough. My pussy feels soft. My clit pulses with tiny detonations of silky warmth, which throb lightly against his hard, colossal thickness. *God help me.*

"You want me." His voice is gruff and I can't help it: I love the sound of it. The deep gravel-edged tone of it seems to reach inside me, stoking the fire.

"No," I lie, gripping his muscular arm. I need something to hold on to. I need him to anchor me.

"I can feel how much you want me," he purrs. "How sweet and wet and ready you are."

"I'm not," I insist.

He nudges his cock harder against the cradling softness of my body. *God*, my pussy is so wet that his gargantuan length slides, displacing the ruined shred of my panties, so my sensitive flesh is rubbed directly against the rough texture of his jeans. "You're going to give yourself to me, baby. Everything."

"No," I manage to breathe. "I can't."

"You can. You will. Let's bet on it. You're going to surrender to me and fall in love with me and give me everything I want, before the month is done. I'll bet my half of the bar on it."

"No." *Why would he do that?* I gasp, because he presses against me again, rolling the tiny bud of my clit with his gigantic cock. *I'm going to come if he keeps doing that.* I try to squirm away from him but it only makes the pleasure spike, so much that I go still, because if either of us moves, I'm going to die of both ecstasy and embarrassment. I'm breathing hard and my heart is thumping in my chest. "I'm not betting you. That's a terrible idea and you're a terrible person for even suggesting it. I'm not giving you anything. Let me go."

"It's not safe for us to move yet." Burning me with the fever in his eyes. Not caring at all that I just called him a terrible person. Which he is. *Very* terrible. "It's a one-sided bet. If you win you can still keep your half." His voice is rasped when he murmurs in my ear, "You want to hear what I'd do first?"

"No."

"I'd peel off this little dress, like I've done in my fantasies. Like in the dreams I've been tormented by since the minute I saw you. Then I'd lay you back on a big, comfortable bed with a view of the ocean and the windows open to let in the breeze and the sun so your perfect skin will be warm to my touch. Then I'd start licking my way down your body."

"Stop," I gasp. I need him to stop talking. His low, deep voice is touching me with its husky allure, funneling its way deep into the low pit of my stomach, and lower, to my sensitive nub, like an electric current is touching me there. My pussy gets even wetter. I can feel the slippery quiver of my inner muscles as my clit throbs gently against the rock-hard ridge of his gigantic cock. The pleasure rises higher and I grip him with both hands, willing myself to keep control of it.

I'm going to come. I don't know if I can stop it from happening.

"You want to hear what I'd do next?"

I can't even reply to him. One word, one breath, and it could all unravel. So I stay very, very still.

"I'd take those little cherry-ripe nipples that I can see under your clothes and I'd suck them into my greedy mouth. One, then the other. I'd suck hard, rolling them with my fingers until they're pink and sore, feasting until I get my fill. I'd get them all messy and wet, until you're almost coming."

Damn him! Can he tell I'm riding a wave that's already too high and too good to slow down?

"And then," he growls softly, "I'll lick my way down to your sweet, wet, pink pussy."

Oh, God.

"I'd lick you slowly, at first. Opening you to me. Taking my time. I'd push my tongue inside you where you'll be saturated with honey that's all for me. Fuck, I'm so *hungry*, baby. I'd eat you like a sweet, juicy fruit until you're begging for me to suck your clit and make you come hard. But I wouldn't do it. Not yet. I'd tease you, swirling my tongue as I slide my fingers inside your tight, wet pussy. Playing you for my own pleasure. And just when you think you might go mad with need, I'll latch onto your clit and suck on your sweet little pussy until you're moaning my name and coming all over my tongue. And then, just as you're starting to come down from all that, I'd slide my—"

I make a low sound, like a sigh.

Oh, God.

Oh, no.

No.

It's happening.

It's happening.

Just from his scent and his grip and his gruff, dirty words.

He pulls me harder against his big body.

He knows. He knows exactly what he's doing.

His cock rubs against my slick, hyper-sensitive clit. He does it again. And again. The pleasure crests in an unbearable swell. Wrenching, hot, out-of-control spasms wrack through my entire body. I curl against him, clinging to his shirt, making a low moan as my pussy clenches tightly, over and over. The rush is so powerful I have tears in my eyes. And as I slowly return to myself I'm crying for more than one reason.

"Hey," Gage smiles gently, tipping my chin up with

his finger. He wipes a tear with his thumb. "You're okay, sweetheart. Everything's good."

Everything's good.

Except that everything's *not* good.

Even if that was very, very good.

I want to push him away but I can't move. I feel overwhelmed by a physical euphoria that's making me feel even more drunk than the whiskey.

We hear a yell outside the door. *All clear.* The noise has died down.

Gage carefully places me on my feet. "Can you stand?" he says softly.

"Yes." *Almost.*

"Can you walk?"

"Yes." *Maybe.*

"Do you want me to carry you?"

"No." *Yes. No. I wish I never met you.*

He smooths my dress and my hair. He licks his thumb and wipes away what might be a smear of my mascara.

"I'm going to hold your hand so I can make sure we're not separated."

"Okay."

Then he pulls his jacket closed and buttons it. His hard-on is—not that I can do more than graze it with my tear-blurred peripheral vision—is…freaking *massive.*

It's a relief to know I'll never be on the receiving end of it.

Because what just happened is as far as this will ever

go. I've experienced his endowments to die for as much as I'm going to.

It's too much.

I *am* broken. And I can't stand to feel any more of him, physically or emotionally. Because he's right. I *will* fall in love with him. And he'll leave, like he did to all the others.

Even as he unlocks the door and grasps my hand in his, I know I absolutely can't allow that to happen. I can't get past the truth: it would devastate me to love him. He'd condemn me to a life of jealousy and the constant fear of betrayal. And I refuse to walk the same road my mother did.

12

The bar has cleared out. The band is long gone. Gage leads me toward the back door that leads out to the alley but I slip my hand from his. "I don't want to ride in the limo."

Watching my face, he takes my hand again. I think he can tell that I mean it, so he starts leading me toward the front door, which is now propped open with several police officers standing outside.

I don't want to be alone with him in a sealed-in space. I don't trust myself. And I don't trust *him*, with his big hard-on and his magnetic, magical power.

Because the thing is—and I'd never in a million years admit this to another person, not even Josie—I've never had an orgasm before the one Gage just gave me.

I've sometimes wondered if, on the occasional lonely night when the urge became hot and unbearable, I'd…

given myself one. It's not something I do often because I don't actually know how—also something I'd never admit to anyone. Sure, I've read Cosmo and Fifty Shades of Grey, but those didn't really answer my questions.

Most days and nights I've been too busy to worry about it. I work long hours and collapse into bed every night, exhausted. Then I sleep for eight hours, get up and sweat and meditate my angst out through yoga, and get on with my job.

So it's not something I've agonized about all that much.

But I *have* wondered.

And now I know for sure.

Nothing has even been in the same galaxy as what just happened to me.

And now that I *do* know for sure, I'm sure as hell not going to let him do it again. Because it's the kind of thing a girl could get addicted to very, very easily.

The feel of that crazy-big, hot hardness. Imagine if he had unzipped.

No.

Imagine coming that hard with his giant cock deep inside you.

Stop, Luna.

The look in his eyes. His face. The current of tenderness swirling through that masculine, savage lust.

Stop it right now, Luna.

It's not happening.

You will remain cool and aloof. You will put up with

him for exactly one month, safeguarding a professional distance. Your business will be transformed—and do not dwell on that insane bet, which I'm sure he'd never deliver on anyway—and you will get on with your life. You will not be destroyed by a man without scruples who's only after one thing and once he gets it, disappears without so much as a backwards glance. He's a genius at what he does, you can admit that much. And recognize it for what it is. You will not crave or obsess about what just happened or how ludicrously good it felt. At all.

There. Decision made.

We walk out onto the street. It's buzzing with the excitement of the secret concert, the breach, the police raid. I overhear enough passing conversations to figure out that people drove in from as far away as Virginia to try to get in to the show tonight. The streets are swarming with hopefuls who were turned away or who spent three packed-in minutes with superstars. There's an air of excitement.

Gage's phone rings and he pulls it out of his pocket. He puts in on speaker. It's Travis. "You guys make it out okay?"

"Yeah, we're fine," Gage tells him. "Everyone still in one piece?"

"Vaughn got his shirt ripped off and Roxie's a little shaken but we're okay. That got way out of control."

"Sure did. You guys might need to stick to stadiums for a while."

Travis's low laugh is almost regretful. "Yeah. It's too bad. I like the small shows best."

"I've got one in mind for you if you're interested. At the end of next month. It's a little venue right here in Key West. I could help with security. We could beef it way up. And we could do more to keep it under wraps. What are you guys doing for New Year's?"

"We kept it free."

"Well, think about it. I'll send you the details."

"Cool, bro. You should come to Nashville for Christmas. We could finally have that reunion we keep talking about."

"Yeah, I'll see."

"Good luck with the new business. She's fucking gorgeous, by the way."

Gage smiles down at me, still holding my hand. "Yeah, I know. And thanks."

Wow. To think that Travis Tucker and his investment prodigy cousin—who also happens to be a GQ cover model and who *also* happens to have just given me a supernova of an orgasm that basically blew my mind—are discussing me like this is…bizarre. Things like this don't happen to me. I'm usually too busy making sure they *don't* happen to me.

I feel dazed.

We walk a little further and I'm glad to have Gage's hand to hold onto. I feel woozy and unsteady. In fact, the further we walk the more drunk I seem to be getting. I should know better than to drink champagne and then pound two shots of Jack on an empty stomach. The endorphin rush—which is, to be honest, epic—isn't helping.

The last thing I want to do is faint or stumble or need rescuing by Doctor O over here.

"Gage, I might go and sit on the beach for a while. You don't need to come with me. I like chilling out on the beach at night sometimes. I can make my own way home. I had fun tonight. Thanks for the ticket."

He laughs, and holds my hand tighter when I try to pull it free. A lock of his hair has fallen across his forehead, somehow adding to his rogue, cavalier beauty in a way that quite literally stuns me. "I'll come with you." Like there's no alternative.

I don't know if I *want* him to come with me. I feel reckless and out of control.

But it's a public beach and there are a lot of people milling around, enjoying their holiday weekend. It's not like we'll be alone.

We get down to the sand and I take off my shoes. "I love Key West sugar sand," I tell him. "There's something so enchanting about it, don't you think? It feels like fairy dust."

He doesn't reply, he just watches me with that steady, riveted intensity he has.

We get to the far end of the beach where there's a cluster of palm trees and no other people. I sit down on the sand and Gage sits next to me. It's a warm, clear night and the stars are out.

They're spinning.

The silence settles around us and it doesn't feel awkward or heavy this time. The gentle sound of the waves on the sand and the faraway laughter filters through it.

"What holds you back?" Gage asks softly in his deep, baritone drawl as he weaves his fingers through mine. "What are you afraid of?"

His hair is dark and thick, curling lightly against his collar from the humidity. The starlight and the moon on the water only amplify the blue glow of his eyes and the intent, open compassion that has nothing to do with the places he's been or the life he's led: it's mine. He's saved this piece of himself just for me. I don't know how I know that but I do.

He's shining his blue light into the cracks in my soul, igniting dark, impossible-to-reach places.

Which is not a good thing. Because I've drunk too much, I've just had one of the most intense experiences of my life and I tend to talk too much even at the best of times. "You," I hear myself confessing. "I'm afraid of you."

"Why?"

"Because you'll hurt me."

"Why do you think I'll hurt you?"

"It's just who you are. And I don't want to be hurt like that."

"What if I told you I wouldn't hurt you."

"You'd be lying."

He doesn't answer right away. "What if I *promised* I wouldn't hurt you?"

"You'd end up breaking your promise."

"Tell me what happened to you."

I blink at him. "How do you know something happened to me?"

"I have a brother who suffers from PTSD. I know the signs."

Damn it. I feel the sting again behind my eyes. "I don't have PTSD. I've never been to war."

"You don't have to go to war to suffer from things that have been extremely difficult in your life. Most people have emotional scars of one kind or another."

I guess that's true. "What are your scars?"

He's quiet for a few seconds. Then, as though he's just made the decision to be honest with me, he says, "My mother died slowly and horribly from pancreatic cancer. My father couldn't live without her and hung himself a month after we lost her."

A tear draws a warm line down my cheek. "I'm so sorry, Gage."

He rubs his fingers along the soft surface of my arm like he's fascinated by the feel of it. "It was a long time ago."

"How long?"

"Five years. I sort of lost control, I think, after it happened. I tried to block it all out by…getting my fix wherever I could. I medicated with money and sex."

Wow. Psychology is pretty interesting. The things people do and why they would. "Did it help?"

"Not really."

A group of people walk past and keep walking. We wait until their voices fade away.

"I want to know what happened to you," he says. "So I can help fix it."

I don't know why I even admit it. "You can't fix it. Josie couldn't. I can't. I don't know why you could."

"Does Josie know what happened?"

"Josie was there through all of it."

"Did you talk about it?"

"What do you mean?"

"Did you get therapy or talk through the things that happened with Josie or anyone else?"

"No. I don't like talking about it."

"That's how I know I can help. It's the talking that breaks it loose. Once it's loose you can start to heal."

I stare at him. "How do you know that? And why do you want to heal me anyway?"

"Because I think I could make you happy and I'd like you to let me try."

Here he goes again. "Gage—"

"My parents met at a party their junior year of

college. My father said he looked at her once and his world literally slid off its axis. That's the way he described it. I always thought he was crazy, of course. I knew for a fact there was no way anything like that could ever happen to me. It's ridiculous, to think you can know something that fast, or that instantly. I used to tell him you can't know a person from one glance."

"You did?"

"Yes. And you know what he said?"

"What?"

"That you can never really know a person. You can only try and have faith and give the best of yourself. That's what he did and she never let him down. Not once. She just kept on amazing him every single day."

I look up at a bright star, which becomes two. "Wow." They swirl around each other like they're dancing. *Maybe it's them,* is what I find myself thinking. "I guess some people just get lucky."

"Or they make their own luck."

"Maybe."

A light breeze touches his hair. He takes off his jacket and gently drapes it over my shoulders. I shiver from the comforting heat of it and the scent of his body. *God, he smells good. Like warmth and wishes and whiskey.* He takes my hand again. "Tell me who it was."

"Who what was?"

"The person who hurt you."

Is he really asking me about this? I sigh and it feels heavy, like it's coming from a mired, long-buried place.

"Did it happen in high school?"

God, why's he so curious? When all my defenses are down? Against every shred of common sense I possess, which at this point in time has been all but obliterated, I hear myself say, "Yes."

"A boyfriend?"

His persistence has slid past some barrier in me. "He was never really a boyfriend. More of a crush. He was the starting quarterback."

His expression as I confess this detail makes me feel like he's *getting* things, piecing things together. And I realize I was wrong about him. He's not cold, not at all. He's one of the most complicated, *feeling* men I've ever met. You just have to get past that hard surface to find it. "That's why you reacted the way you did in the limo, when I told you I used to play quarterback."

I shrug lightly.

"So you had a crush on the quarterback. What happened next?"

"Everyone had a crush on the quarterback. I'm sure you know all about it."

"People get crushes on all kinds of people all the time. Did you date him?"

Did I date him. An interesting question. "I don't think you could call it a date."

"You went out with him."

"Once."

"Tell me what happened."

I guess sometimes when someone makes a request into a donut hole of a perfectly vulnerable moment, it's possible to eke out an answer. "It was a party. A pool party, the first week of school, at a senior's house. I was a junior and all the football players were there and we went along. Me and Josie and a few other people."

"He noticed you and started talking to you."

"Yes."

"You had a crush on him. And one thing led to another." Of course he knows the story. He probably has a thousand stories like this, told from the other point of view.

I can't answer. This was a terrible idea.

"Luna, it's okay. Keep going. Once it's out, it'll feel a lot lighter."

I mean, what the hell. Maybe he's right. I'll feel lighter and he'll go back to Chicago and I'll never have to see him again. "We were drinking this punch they gave us. And he invited me upstairs to a room where there were a lot of football players. But then they all left and it was just us. And then…" *God. Why am I telling this story to him, of all people?*

His voice is low. "Did you consent to it? Or not?"

"I don't know. I had a crush on him. Everyone did. He was the guy every girl wanted. And he wanted *me*. I was seventeen and a lot of my friends already had boyfriends and were talking about the things they were doing and…I wasn't really expecting *everything* but he was very pushy and…anyway, I went with it. It happened." More tears are wetting my face. We're this deep in anyway, so I keep going. "I cried because…I don't know. It doesn't matter now. He didn't seem to notice that part of it and when we went back downstairs all his friends laughed and teased him because…they all knew. I understood then that he did this all the time. Every weekend. I wasn't special or chosen, I was just one of many. A conquest now conquered, before he moved on to the next one. Of course I wished I could undo it, but I couldn't. So I didn't let it devastate me, even though I'd expected something a little more…meaningful, maybe. A lot of people do, though, right? There's nothing unusual about that. So I got on with my life." He waits. I'm sure he can tell there's more to this story. He doesn't push. He just holds my hand as I stare out at the water. So I keep talking. "But then, about six weeks later I realized I was…late."

As soon as I say it, I wildly regret it. I regret all of this. I regret not fighting harder to change Josie's mind about signing that damn contract. And I fully expect Gage to disengage, to say goodnight, to walk up the beach and jump on the first private jet back to Chicago. Why would someone like him want to hear about something like this from someone like me?

Instead of skirting around the subject squeamishly, he grabs it by the horns. "He got you pregnant."

The tears are streaming now. The dancing stars are blurry. Gage puts a clean handkerchief in my hand and I use it to wipe my eyes.

"Did he step up?"

"Step up? If you call handing me a crumpled wad of dollar bills and telling me to 'take care of it,' then yes, he really stepped up. He wasn't interested. He answered my call once but he threatened to deny everything if I tried to 'corner' him. That's how he put it. I later found out this wasn't the first time this had happened to him. We were just collateral damage to his fun, 'alpha' lifestyle. But I couldn't bring myself to do it. Even though I knew I couldn't care for a baby—I mean, I could barely care for myself—I just couldn't do it. I made my decision and I was going to keep the baby and figure everything out along the way, somehow. By then, people knew. The school found out. It was a small, conservative place and my dirty secret became exactly that. Everyone treated me differently, which seemed kind of amazing in this day and age, but they did. People avoided me and bullied me on social media. The country club mothers didn't want their daughters hanging around me because I was a bad influence—while *he* got congratulated. I was told to stay home and finish high school online because of the 'backlash' but none of it tarnished his star, not one bit. I was scared and alone. But Billy Burke was a hero for slaying girls all over town."

"Billy Burke. I know that name. He played two seasons for Notre Dame."

"Did he?" I'd made a point of *not* following his career.

"He was their up-and-coming golden boy before his neck was fractured in a bad tackle made in the final few seconds of the playoffs. He never made it to the NFL."

"Good." I'm not a vengeful person on the whole but I'm glad to hear he fell off his pedestal.

"What happened next?" As Gage asks me the question, he does the most outrageous thing. He smooths my hair with his rough hand, so, so gently. He's not scared of this, or disapproving, or disgusted. And I can just tell by the staunchness of him in this moment—even though I can't know for sure, I somehow just *do*—that Gage hasn't done the things I'm describing. That he *would* have stepped up, or not let it happen the way it did in the first place. His women cry because it's so *good*, not because it's so…awful. Because it was. It was painful and scary and heartbreaking. And it succeeded in making sure I wanted nothing to do with it again for a very long time.

"A few weeks later I…I lost the baby. I wasn't very far along and it just happens sometimes, they said. And I was even more sad, after that, because I was just so incredibly *relieved*. I felt terrible, and guilty, for feeling that way. But I was."

"Of course you were relieved. There's no shame in that. Where were your parents through all this?"

"Gone. Never there in the first place. My parents were the kind of parents who never parented. They never pretended to want to. My father was busy philandering his way through Westchester County and my mother was living the dream—or the nightmare, depending on your perspective—in the Hollywood Hills. I never told them any of it. It wouldn't have helped. I leaned on Josie. But I was already living in her house with her brothers and her dad, who were kind and they might have known but…you know, it's not the kind of thing you talk about over dinner."

"No, it wouldn't be."

Gage was right about one thing: I do feel lighter. Exhausted and…empty. Tears wet my face. "I'm sorry for telling you all this, Gage. Really. There's nothing fun or glamorous or romantic about it and I didn't mean to ruin your night. I'm so sorry."

"You haven't ruined my night, sweetheart. Shit happens, all the time, to all of us. It's called life, and most of it is fucking brutal. You didn't do anything wrong. You were young and some asshole took advantage of you and it was hard and it's still hard. But it doesn't define who you are and you shouldn't let it. Think about all the good things that have happened since then. You've achieved a lot for someone so young. You own a business. And I'm sure you've met nicer guys since then and had some better experiences."

"No. I mean…no. I just…couldn't." God, it's so embarrassing.

"What do you mean?"

"I haven't…that was the only—"

"Wait a minute." He stares at me in disbelief. "Do you mean to tell me you've never been with anyone else since that happened?"

"No. Not…until…well, tonight. And that was the first —" No. I can't tell him that. This is too crazily awkward. *God, I wish I could take it all back like I've never wished for anything.*

He watches my eyes, like he's deeply affected by what I've just told him. "Well, that's just not right."

I don't know if it's right or not. I suddenly feel incredibly drained. Confessing all this has left me weary to the bone. Gage seems to sense that.

He pulls his phone out of his jacket pocket. "I'm going to message my driver—no protests—and have him pick up a couple of burgers for us. You're going to eat something and I'm going to take you home. You're going to get a good night's sleep. And then I want to see you again tomorrow."

I've just told my deepest, darkest, most personal secret to this gorgeous glitterati guru playboy. I know that as soon as the whiskey has worn off I'm going to feel mortified and deeply humiliated. I can already feel the remorse creeping in. "I'm helping Josie pack tomorrow and then I have to work. I want to spend this time with her since we won't see each other again for a while. She's leaving at four on Sunday afternoon. I'll go to the airport with her. Then I've got a yoga class at six. So I won't be able to see you again this weekend."

I don't want to see him again. At all. I've already decided that. I don't even want to co-own a business with him.

I don't know what I want to do. Maybe I'll go somewhere else for a while and let him take care of the upgrades on his own. Maybe I'll go to New Orleans. Or Austin. I don't know. Right now, I just feel tired.

"I'd like you to let me take care of your ride to the airport and back," he says. "Josie will have a lot of stuff, I imagine. You might as well take the limo. I'll have the driver pick you up at two thirty."

I start to refuse but Josie would *love* that. "Sure. Thanks."

I follow his gaze to the edge of the beach where the limo is already pulling up. "I'm going to pick you up and carry you. You're tired and I don't want you falling over or hurting yourself. I'll be careful with you. Okay?"

I don't have it in me to argue with him. I don't think I've ever been this exhausted in my life. "Okay."

He *is* careful with me. He carries me across the sand and places me on the back seat of the limo like I'm made of fine china. He feeds me some fries. I eat a few bites of a hamburger but I'm not hungry.

We don't say much on the way back to the bar. The moving lights of Key West outside the tinted windows paint his face in shifting colors as he watches me. If you asked me to judge him on this moment alone, I'd never in a million years guess he was anything but a beautiful soul.

The limo pulls up outside the bar. "Gage," I say, before he can jump out. "You don't need to walk me in or carry me. I'm fine. Please. Please stay here." I feel like if he touches me again I might shatter.

He obeys me, unhappily.

"Goodnight, Gage."

"Goodnight, Luna. You'll feel better. I promise."

I can feel him watching me as I make my way inside. I don't bother looking back.

Somehow I make it up the stairs. I let my ruined dress fall to the floor and I crawl into my bed, pulling the covers over my head.

Holy hell. Way to ruin an evening, Luna.

It's good. It's best this way. Now he'll never want anything to do with you.

Sleep washes over me. The dark oblivion of it has never felt so good.

13

———

GAGE

I can't handle this.

I don't recognize myself.

Damn everything to hell.

Did *I* leave a trail of wreckage and sadness?

No. I can honestly say that I've gone out of my way *not* to do that. I've slept with a lot of women. And I always made sure every single one of them knew exactly what they were getting into. I made sure they laughed and understood that it was about sex and only sex. Consent has never been an issue—and I made sure of it. It's usually them hunting me down and me going with it. Their anger was about wanting *more* of what I gave them. I have never in my life had sex without a condom. And they were condoms *I* provided, in case any of them got any tricky ideas.

I want to fix her. I want to make everything okay again. I want to heal her and show her how beautiful she is. I want to make her feel good and whole and fully alive. I want to show her that, even though we all have things that have happened to us that change us and cut us down, it doesn't mean we can't be happy anyway.

That's what I'm going to do.

Starting right now, I'm going take everything I've ever done—and everything anyone else has ever done—and make it all up to her.

Luna isn't the only one with regrets.

Life is messy. And painful. It hurts sometimes. It's hard not to get overwhelmed.

She coped by closing a part of herself off, for good reason. I've coped with my own demons by becoming cold. Hard. By behaving like an asshole a lot of the time, I know that. I'm *aware* that I'm doing it *as* I'm doing it. But the thing is, I'm not *actually* an asshole. Deep down there's as much of the good stuff as my parents had, they made sure of it.

I buried the good stuff for a long time. I was angry at myself for feeling too much. I wanted to crush my emotions any way I could.

I don't want to do that anymore.

I'm done. Just like that.

All it took was a glance, her perfect face, a dismissal, a yellow dress, *a white dress*, a dance, a locked-away moment that was the most beautiful thing that's ever happened to me, and a painful confession.

Now I know why she's scared.

I've known many people like him, of course I have. I was a part of that scene, to a certain extent.

But I'm not him. I'm nothing like him and I never was.

Now all I need to do is convince her of that.

All the hard, heartless, I-don't-give-a-fuck years have led me here. To a place where I understand how much I've been missing out on.

All my raging, misdirected energy has converged into one white-hot fireball of obsession that has lodged itself right in the middle of my chest. I'm going to heal her and give her everything she's ever dreamed of. I'm going to replace one innocent mistake and all its painful consequences with a lifetime of good memories.

Am I in love with her?

Can a person know for sure, so quickly, so suddenly?

As much as a person can ever know.

I do. I fucking *love* her.

I'm completely and utterly besotted with her.

I feel like fucking crying. And laughing. I feel like getting drunk and howling at the moon. I feel like breaking my way into her apartment and crawling into bed with her, wrapping myself around that sweet little body and soul and holding her close. Making sure she's warm enough. Make sure she's not scared anymore. Making her smile and come and laugh like she's never laughed.

It's a gargantuan shift. *Like the world is tilting off its axis.*

My life has suddenly taken on a new meaning. It's not about what *I* want anymore. It's about what will make her happy enough to let me in. Her smile is more important to me than my own has ever been.

Fucking hell.

This is intense.

I get my driver to pull over. I get out and walk for a while. I think about what I'm going to do. I start to make a plan. I need to keep myself occupied or I'll never last two whole days without fucking running over there and banging down her door.

Women check me out as I walk along the waterfront, like they always do.

Fuck off! I feel like yelling. *I'm hers. I finally found her. She exists! She's perfect and she's real. Everything about me belongs to her and only her.*

Should I go to her now?

No. I'll give her the weekend to say her goodbyes to Josie and to sleep off the release of a long-held, painful confession. My mother used to go to therapy. She always used to go to bed after a session and sleep for several hours. Right now I'm in the process of finding someone for Caleb to see. I know enough about psychology to understand that Luna is probably going to be dealing with some pretty heavy emotions this weekend. It's good she's with Josie. Josie knows. Josie will soften the pain with her kindness and the comforting depth of their long friendship.

Come Monday morning, though, baby, you're all mine.

So I go back to my hotel suite.

I spend the next fifty-four hours, eighteen minutes and twelve seconds doing research, making phone calls, falling into fitful black holes of sleep that she haunts with her sighs and her softness. I crave her like a man possessed. I love her so much it feels like the memory of her and the promise of seeing her again are rearranging the alchemy of my soul.

I almost break down a hundred times.

I decide to send her flowers. She won't mind that, will she?

I do it. I send four dozen roses and a few other things she might like. I try not to go overboard. I don't want to overwhelm her but if I don't do *something* that touches her I'm seriously going to lose my goddamn fucking mind.

I work out in the private gym for a while. I do a few laps in the pool. I order room service and get drunk and, for the very first time, I cry over the death of my parents. *I get it now,* I tell them. *I get everything. I found it. I found her.*

When I wake up, I feel better. Like I promised Luna *she* would, I feel lighter. The dark and twisted edges of me are colored with singular intent. Her. I'm going to replace her fear with beauty. I'm going to wash away her sadness with pleasure. I'm going to get her to fall in love with me by loving her so much she'll have no other choice.

14

"WHY ARE YOU SO QUIET?" Josie asks me as I help her pack up her three mammoth suitcases. "You said you had fun last night, aside from the stampede."

"I did."

"Did something happen?"

"No, not at all." I haven't told Josie what Gage and I talked about. Or…the other stuff. I don't want to worry her. She's got enough to deal with. "I'm thinking about taking a vacation."

"What kind of vacation?"

"I've never been to New Orleans. I've always wanted to go there. All these years I've lived in Florida, which isn't even that far, and I've never been there. It doesn't seem right." The words he'd used. *Now that's just not right.*

"You should take a couple days off and go there."

"Yeah. I think I will. On Monday."

"Monday?" She studies me for a few seconds. "Luna, did something happen between you and Gage last night?"

"No. I told you, we met the band and danced a little and then the breach thing happened and then…once we could get out we sat on the beach for a while and talked and then I came home."

"What did you talk about?"

I almost brush it off, but my hesitation gives me away. She knows something's up, so I just tell her. "I drank more than I meant to and he was asking a lot of questions. And he somehow got me talking about…what happened to me. I told him everything. I'm so embarrassed." There's not even any warning: I burst into tears.

Josie comes over and gives me a hug. A long one. One that doesn't ask questions or judge. "It's okay, Loon. Everything's okay. If he got you to talk about that he must have been very kind about it. He must have made you feel like you could trust him."

Had he? Maybe he had. "I'm sure he'll want to keep his distance now."

She holds my shoulders, pulling back. "Why would you say that?"

"Because. I'm damaged."

"Jesus, Luna, would you stop with the 'damaged.' You really need to change your narrative. There's nothing *damaged* about you. You're kind and smart and successful and gorgeous. So you had a bad experience once, who hasn't? Look at me."

"But that wasn't a bad experience."

"No, it was an exceptionally *good* experience. Which makes the whole thing worse, because I'll never have it again. And *now* who's going to want me? With two crazy little boys thrown into the deal. Because I can already tell they're going to be a handful." She places her hand on her stomach. "They're either going to be soccer players or acrobats."

"Plenty of guys will want you, Josie. You're beautiful."

"And *you're* beautiful. Inside and out. If Gage McCabe is scared off by what you told him last night then he's not a man you'd want anyway."

"I never really thought about it that way before."

She hands me a box of tissues. "Well, it's time you did. Way *past* time you did. It's time for you to get back on that horse, girl. Or get on the horse to begin with, more accurately."

I take a deep breath. "I know. You're right."

"Of course I'm right," she says gently. "This is good. Now you can *finally* start to move on."

I take a tissue and dry my face. "I've cried more in the past day than I have in the past five years."

"Welcome to the club."

There's a loud pounding on the downstairs door.

"Luna!" Rico yells. "There's a delivery here for you."

"Delivery?" I walk toward the door. "I'll go see what it is."

I go downstairs and open the door into the restaurant.

There's a deliveryman there with…a lot of flowers. And packages. "What is this?"

"Are you Luna LaRoux?"

"Yes."

"Where do you want this stuff?"

"What is it? Who's it from?"

"It doesn't say. You want it upstairs?"

"Uh…yeah. Okay."

I pick up one of the enormous bouquets as the man carries several boxes, wrapped in brown paper, and a large envelope. He has to make several trips.

I close the door behind him.

Josie touches a perfect red rose and sniffs it. "Wow. These are beautiful."

There's a card attached to one of the bouquets. She reads it out. "'Luna, here are some of the things you'll need as we get started with the upgrades. There's something for Josie too. I hope you're having a good weekend. See you on Monday. ~G'" Josie searches through the packages. "I get one too?" She finds the package with her name on it and rips open the wrapping. "It's a brand new iPad," she gasps. "It's the newest model."

A card falls from the box. Josie opens it and begins to read it to me. "'Josie. This is for you, so you and Luna can keep in close contact. The passcode is 1234 until you change it. The device has been loaded with a few extra apps you might find useful. I hope you'll forgive me: I asked Luna and pried an answer out of her. And I hope you'll forgive me, too, for taking the liberty, but I thought you might like to know that there were six different men with the first name of Noah who used California-based bank cards in Key West between the dates of April 1 and June 30. Their photographs and details are included in the file labeled NOAH. If you'd prefer to delete it unopened there are no other copies. Please let me know if I can be helpful. See you soon, hopefully, and all the best with your new family. Gage.'" Josie is still staring at the card. "He asked you about it?"

"Yes. I'm sorry I told him, sweetie."

"I'm *glad* you told him, Luna. I can't believe he searched."

Carefully, I ask her, "Do you want to look at the file?"

"Of course I do!" She pulls my arm and we go together to sit on the couch by the window.

She enters the passcode and there it is. The file titled NOAH.

Josie takes a deep breath. "I'm going to look now, Luna. Are you ready?"

I laugh. "Ready as I'll ever be." I link my arm through hers.

She taps on the file. The first photo that pops up is of a man with dark hair, probably in his 60s. "Well, that's not him." Josie scrolls down to the next one. "This isn't him either."

"Keep going."

She scrolls past the third. And the fourth. To the fifth.

And there he is. Blond hair. Green eyes. Handsome, suntanned face. "Luna. *It's him.*" Josie reads from the information listed under his driver's license. "Noah Alexander Walker. Occupation: architect. Address: 4912 Oceanview Lane, Big Sur, California."

I keep reading. "He's single, he drives a Jeep Cherokee and he has a dog named Whiskey. How would Gage even find all that out?"

"*God.* Luna. Do you think I should contact him?"

"I think you should do whatever feels right to you, honey."

She squeezes my hand. "At least he's not married, according to this."

"What are you going to do?"

"His phone number is listed here. And his email address."

"Think about it. Let it settle. If it feels right, you can contact him when you're ready."

"I need to figure out what to say. I don't want him to feel obligated or anything. It's a pretty big deal to find out you're about to become the father of twins, right? I don't want him to feel like I'm asking him to do anything, or give us anything. I don't *need* him."

"No. You just want to let him know. In case he wants to…" I almost say *step up*, but catch myself, "…be a part of their lives, if that's what you want. That's what you need to think about, Josie. Do you want him to be a part of their lives?"

"I think he should have that choice. He's their *father*."

"Yes. He is."

Josie stares at Noah's photo for what might be a full minute. She zooms in. "He's so beautiful," she whispers. "I wonder if they'll look like him."

"Probably a little bit."

We're laughing and crying at the same time. "Luna, I want to call him now."

"Now?"

"Yes. I don't want to wonder or overthink it. I just want to let him know and then he can react however he's going to react."

"Are you sure?"

"Yes. What time is it in California right now?"

"It's 1:28 here. So it must be 10:28 in the morning."

"It's Saturday. It's a good time."

"Okay. Wow. Josie, do you…do you want some privacy? I can wait in my room for a while."

"No. I'm going to call him and put him on speaker-phone. I need you here, Luna."

"Okay. Of course. If that's what you want."

Josie picks up her phone.

"My heart's beating so fast right now," I whisper.

"Mine too. The babies are going crazy in there." She brings up the keypad on her phone. She takes a deep breath. "Here goes nothing." She keys in Noah's number.

He answers on the third ring. "Hello?"

"Noah? Hi, it's Josie Farrell calling. We met one night in Key West around six months ago."

Silence. "Oh. Yeah. Hi." He doesn't sound mad or spooked or caught off guard. He sounds sort of neutral. Sort of nice.

"I'm sorry to call you out of the blue like this," Josie says, "but I wanted to get in touch. I searched for you, I hope you don't mind. Because, well, there's no easy way to say this but I wanted to let you know—and I'll start by telling you that I'm not asking for anything, not at all. I don't need anything. But after we spent that night together, which was really a beautiful night, by the way, just saying…" Josie falters a little so I squeeze her hand and she keeps going. "I found out a few weeks later that… well, I'm pregnant. With twins."

A shocked silence. "What?"

"Yeah. And…I mean, I haven't been with anyone else in around a year or so…I'm sorry, I know this is very unexpected. It was for me too. And as I said, I'm not asking for anything. I just wanted to let you know because it felt like the right thing to do. And…well, you have my number in your phone now so if you ever want to call me or find out about anything or—"

"When are you due?"

Josie seems a little shocked, that he would ask this, or that he hasn't hung up yet. "Oh. In February. They're boys. Twin boys."

Another long silence. "Wow," he says.

"Yeah," Josie agrees.

"Are you okay?" Noah asks and—*holy hell, here I go again.* Tears are streaming down my face. *He cares. He absolutely cares.*

Josie doesn't answer right away. She's not crying. She seems suddenly…stronger. "I'm okay. Once I got over the shock, it's been easier. The doctor says I'm healthy and the babies are growing well. I'm leaving for Iowa tomorrow. It's where my family is."

"Iowa, huh. My uncle lives in Iowa City."

"Oh. Well, that's not too far from where I'll be."

There's another long silence before he says, "Josie?"

"Yeah?"

"I'm really glad you called me."

"You are?"

"Yeah. I've thought about you a lot."

"You have?"

"Yes."

"I've thought about you a lot too." She laughs a little. I pick up the phone and take it off speaker. I hold it to her ear and she holds it. I squeeze her hand and leave them to it. As I'm closing the door of my bedroom I hear Josie laugh, sort of carefully. She's not getting too hopeful, which is good, but there *is* hope there. A lot of hope. And it's the most beautiful thing in the world, I realize: hope.

I think about my own hopes.

I can't seem to summon many, at all.

The hope section of my brain feels clouded and dark, overshadowed by something else.

Regret.

Not even about what happened so much anymore, but about being so messed up by it. So unable to just let it go. And most of all, right now, I regret crying—*and coming*—and confessing all that to a perfect stranger who no doubt sent me flowers out of sheer pity, for making a long-ago mistake and for not being strong enough to let it go.

It's weird what happens at that exact moment, though: I do let it go.

Suddenly, it happens, just like that.

I forgive myself.

Maybe I *did* need to get it out of my system, as he said.

Once it's loose you can begin to heal.

Maybe Gage was right.

I pick up my phone and search for the Greyhound bus schedule to New Orleans on Monday morning.

It's not really that I don't want to face him.

It's more that I don't want to see him again at all.

Because once I got a glimpse under his cocky arrogance, to the part of him that cared enough to break me wide open, while at the same time smoothing my hair, wiping my tears, putting his warm jacket around me, carrying me and feeding me…*not to mention giving me the* *most outrageously stellar orgasm, my first, which was not just beautiful but life-changing…*this is dangerous territory.

I could fall in love with Gage McCabe.

Maybe I already have.

You have. You totally have.

Damn it.

I can forgive myself once, but not twice.

What if I promised you I'd never hurt you?

You'd end up breaking your promise.

The 7 a.m. bus to New Orleans on Monday is fully booked. There's another one departing at 9:30. I pay for the ticket and book myself a cheap hotel. I'll find a job and a room somewhere. I'll lay low for a month and see how I feel at the end of it. Maybe he'll want to buy me out too, for whatever I own in equity.

I'll leave him a note. I'll give him full reign, which he already has anyway, he made sure of that. So, let him deal with it. The staff rosters are already in place, the place runs like clockwork most days. No doubt he's got his own grand plans for the renovations. He can obviously handle it.

I sleep for a while. Deeply. With no dreams.

Josie and Noah talk for hours. After, she sits on my bed and tells me everything. He wants to see her again. He'll come to Iowa and they'll take it from there. He talked about maybe bringing her and the babies out to Big Sur, where he owns a house he designed, with a view of the ocean. She's not going to get her hopes up, but a weight has been lifted. She doesn't feel quite so alone anymore.

"Luna," she says. "Please tell Gage thank you. So much. I'm so grateful he searched for Noah."

"Of course I will." I don't tell her that I'm leaving for New Orleans before I see him, but I'll make sure to include it in the note.

The next day the limo picks us up, right on time, and I go with Josie to the airport. We hug a lot and promise to FaceTime non-stop and she boards her flight and that's it.

A new chapter.

Me, against the world.

The limo drops me at the bar and I get into my yoga outfit but I never quite make it to my class.

I pack my bag. I'll get an early Uber, I decide. I book one. It's unlikely he'll show up before nine, if at all. Maybe he'll just send a contractor or a project manager at some point during the week. We didn't really talk about that. Whatever. If he's owned forty businesses, he can figure it out.

God, I'm so tired.

I crawl into bed. From here, I can see the water.

I'll miss it here.

But it's best this way.

I stare out at the view, where the moon reflects its light into a shimmery line that stretches all the way to the horizon.

I notice then two stars, close together. Maybe those

same ones. And I remember something Gage said, about the way his father described his mother.

You can never really know a person. You can only try. And hope for the best. That's what he did and she never let him down. Not once. She just kept on amazing him every single day.

God, it must be so romantic and beautiful to love like that.

I scold myself for thinking it but I can't help it.

I wish I could love and be loved like that.

By him.

15

"Luna."

I'm on a soft, sandy beach at sunset. He's calling to me, walking toward me in his business clothes, crossing a divide.

"Luna, honey. Wake up."

I feel movement, next to me. Of something big. And heavy.

"Luna. Wake up, sweetheart. I need to talk to you about something."

My eyes blink open. I peek through a small hole in the cave I've made with my comforter.

"Hey." He's smiling.

Gage is lying next to me with his head on my other pillow, on his side, facing me, arms folded. He's dressed in worn jeans and an old blue t-shirt that hugs his broad shoulders and his defined muscles. In the purple light of dawn, his irises are a pale greenish-blue. Against the white

188

sheets, his skin is dark. His thick dark hair is sticking up in places. He hasn't shaved. *He's mind-numbingly beautiful.* He looks like he hasn't slept much since I saw him last. He blinks his lashes at me.

"What are you doing here?" I whisper.

"I couldn't wait any longer."

"For what?"

"To see you."

"How did you get in?"

"I have a key now, remember?"

"Oh."

"I wanted to make sure you were okay and not too lonely. How'd it go with Josie?"

I pull the comforter down a little, so I can see him more clearly. "Gage, she called Noah. One of those photos was him. They're going to keep in touch and maybe even see each other again. She was so, so happy. Thank you for doing that. She wanted me to thank you."

There's tender gravity in his eyes when he says, "See, some guys do step up."

Damn you. Don't remind me that I spilled my guts to you and you now have even more power over me. This is exactly why I wanted to get away from him. Then I remember. My bus. "What time is it?"

"Six fifteen."

"Six fifteen? Gage, what are you doing here? In my *bed*," I point out.

Not even a hint of contrition. "I'm not *in* it, I'm *on* it."

Outside the window, the indigo sky bleeds crimson along the dark line of the horizon. We gaze at each other in the red-tinted room and it *hurts*. His beauty is quite literally making my heart ache. It's not just the handsomeness of his face or the masculine perfection of his toned, muscular body, it's his expression. He's staring at me almost…worshipfully.

"I needed to see you," he says quietly.

I don't ask it right away. I can almost tell, just by staring into his eyes. "Why?"

"I need to tell you some things."

Gently: "At six fifteen in the morning?"

"Yes."

"Well, all right then. Let's hear it."

"Not yet."

"Not yet?"

"No."

"Why?"

"Because."

I remember the night we danced. "Because isn't an answer." We already have inside jokes.

He smiles lazily. Like he has all the time in the world. "You really want to hear the reason?"

"Well, since you broke into my room at dawn to tell me, it must be important. So, yes."

He looks around my room. "This is a cool space. I like it."

"Thanks."

"Luna." His expression is so hopeful and also so suddenly vulnerable that I can't help it, I feel that glow deep inside myself, stronger this time.

I'm so in love with him.

"This has been the longest fucking weekend of my life," he says huskily.

"It has?"

"Yes. It has. I've been doing a lot of thinking and I want to say some things to you but I don't want you to answer right away, because I know what you're going to say and I want you to give me a chance to say everything I'm going to say first, before you say anything. Okay?"

"Um…"

"Please." He's doing it again, where his swagger lifts at the edges and reveals the more raw, feeling side of his personality. It's not the first time I've seen it—or the first time I've had the strange realization that this part of him is just for me.

"Okay. Go ahead. I'm listening."

"You promise you won't say anything until I'm done talking?"

"I'm not sure why—"

"Just say, 'Gage, I promise I won't interrupt you until you've said what you need to say.'"

I crinkle up my face and laugh a little. Because this is crazy.

"See?" he says. "You're doing it again."

"Doing what?"

"Killing me."

I sit up a little further and lean against the smooth, curved surface of my headboard. I take a drink of water from the glass on my bedside table. I keep the comforter pulled up to my collarbone to cover me. I'm still in my yoga shorts and a tight, cropped tank top. Gage sits up next to me. It's hard to process the magnitude of how over-the-top gorgeous he is, all tousled in his ancient, snug t-shirt and his jeans, which fit him in a way that should be illegal. He's big and sexy and, all of a sudden, so earnest he seems younger and sort of…sweet. His outrageous hotness mixed with this hint of kindness is a lethal combination. Because there's no way in hell I can resist it for long.

I want to kiss him. I want to climb onto him and kiss his insanely beautiful mouth.

But then I'll lose the bar. And he'll have won.

"I'm still waiting," he says. Okay, not *that* sweet.

I obey him because now I'm curious. I want to hear this. "Gage, I promise I won't interrupt you until you've said what you need to say."

"Thank you. All right." He rubs his hand against his square, stubbled jaw. Then his aqua gaze meets mine. He doesn't speak right away and the silence feels loaded. Like it's about to change my life. "Maybe I should wait until later. Let me take you out to breakfast first."

"*Gage.* Just tell me now."

"I'm not sure you're ready."

"I'm *ready.* Just tell me what it is."

He studies me, and then, as though deciding that I'm not ready *enough*, he says, "No."

I give him an exasperated look, then roll my eyes. "You break in to my apartment at six fifteen to wake me up because this *thing* you have to tell me is so important it can't wait and now you're not even going to *tell* me? Fine, I'll just go back to sleep until you—"

"I love you."

I stare at him in mute shock. I gasp lightly.

He holds up a finger, to remind me of my oath. "I know what you're thinking. That I'm insane. *I* think I'm insane so I can only imagine how it sounds to you. But I do. I love you. I *know* I love you because I feel like I've been hit by a fucking lightning bolt right in the middle of my heart. In fact I had a dream that you were *holding* my heart, all bloody, in your hands, and you wanted to give it back to me but I wouldn't take it. You're *still* holding it, that's how it feels. I know how fucked up that sounds but it's true. I've never had anything like this happen to me before—not even fucking close. And I know what you're going to say, that I don't know you well enough to love you. But I don't think it works that way all the time. I think you *can* know. I *know* that I know. And I want you to let me show you. I want to spend time with you. *All* my time. I want to give you things and make you happy, starting now. I don't want to wait and fuck around and pretend that I'm not going mad with lust and with love.

What I realize is that I've been waiting a long time already and I'm *tired* of waiting, like I've been searching but never, ever finding. Until you. That's how it feels. Like I finally fucking *found* you. So I'm going to do everything I can to wow you and win you and get you to fall in love with me. And I know what you think of me, but you're wrong. I can't change who I've been or what I've done in the past, but that's what it is: the past. A different life. A life that made me angry and sort of feral because the whole time I was pissed off that I wasn't worthy of the real thing. The thing everyone aspires to and most of all me—even though I never admitted it to myself. And I don't expect you to love me back right away. I know it'll take time. But I also *know* I can convince you. And I'm grateful to you, honey, for being honest with me the other night, even though I know that was hard for you to do. But I'm glad you told me, so I can understand what hurts you. So I can make sure you don't feel scared anymore. Because that's what I'm going to do. I'm going to treat you like the beautiful goddess you are. I'll be careful with you. I'll take care of you. Starting right now. I waited two whole infinite thousand-hour days to see you again and I couldn't wait another minute."

My heart's beating, not fast, but heavily, thumping with…I don't know. That hope I couldn't find before, maybe. *Is this real?* I can't quite absorb the enormity of what he's confessing to me.

Before I can respond or even react, my phone starts

playing a song. It's the one I use for an alarm, a slow, soulful song about seizing the day by the Tucker Brothers Band. I pick up my phone and touch the screen, which stops the music, but it pings again with an alert. *Uber. 7:30 a.m.*

"Uber?" Gage asks.

"Yeah."

"Where are you going?"

"I…booked a bus ticket."

"To where?"

"New Orleans."

"Today?"

I watch his face for a few seconds. He's staring at me sternly. I nod, just barely, and bite my lip.

He watches me do this. "If I didn't know better I might think you were running away from me."

I don't bother denying that that's exactly what I was about to do.

Gage takes my hand, which is resting on the covers next to me. "I'm not him, honey. You need to know that."

Just two days ago, the mention of *him* would have rocked me to my core. Now, already, it has become a part of our lexicon, something Gage knows about and something we *talk about*. It's jarring but also…therapeutic, weirdly. Having it *out there*, in the air, instead of all cooped up, makes the memory feel much less heavy. "I know. You're you." I almost don't say it but I think about all the things he just confessed, and being honest with him is …

the only way I can be. So I say it quietly. "The most eligible bachelor in Chicago's glitterati dating scene." *But don't expect him to stick around until morning, ladies.* I don't bother saying that last part out loud, but he already knows.

His eyes narrow. "You googled me."

"And you googled me." I grew up in a house where my mother cried all the time and my father barely ever came home. He broke her heart, not just once but all the time. They all did. All her husbands, or at least most of them. "Have you ever been faithful, Gage?"

"I've never *tried* to be faithful. I never had anyone to be faithful *to*."

"What if you can't do it?"

He moves closer, climbing over me, crouching above me like a big cat, holding his weight so he's pinning me in place but not crushing me. Entirely. The power in the hard planes of his body is dizzying.

"What if *you* can't do it?" he asks. "What if we never try and never know? The thing is, Luna, I've never promised anything to anyone. Ever. So I've never had a promise to break. Until now. And I'm promising you this, sweet girl: I won't hurt you. I don't *want* anyone else. I've been waiting my whole life for you to walk into it and slay me with one glance. I was too cynical to believe you ever would, for a long time. But now that you have I'm afraid you're stuck with me, sweetheart. Go ahead and try to run from me. I'll chase after you. I'm going to have to prove myself to you, I know that. And I will. I'll convince you, baby, kiss by kiss. Where should I start, I wonder." Roguishly. A detail of him that's never far from the surface. His eyes are startlingly bright. His hair is wild, his sumptuous mouth beyond tempting.

He leans closer. But I remember, again. The bet.

I place my hand on his chest to stop him. "I'm not kissing you, Gage. I can't." *Because if I do, I'll never be able to stop.*

He spears me with a look. Then it dawns on him. "Did you open the envelope I sent you?"

"No. Josie opened hers but I—"

He climbs off me with the ease of an athlete and lifts me into his arms like I weigh no more than a child. He carries me into the living room.

"Gage—"

"I'll take you to New Orleans this weekend. I own a hotel in the French Quarter."

"You do?"

"Yes. We'll take my jet. I'll book us dinner on a Mississippi riverboat and we'll catch some live music. My favorite jazz club is open all night. But first, you need to open these presents."

He places me on the couch, still wrapped in my comforter. The entire apartment is infused with the heady perfume of the topiary-sized bouquets of roses. Their blooms are the largest I've ever seen. Gage gathers the wrapped packages and the large envelope and puts them on the coffee table. Then he sits next to me, with his arms folded across his brawny chest and a pissed-off scowl on his face. "Start with that one. And no arguing. These are things we'll need for the renovations. I need you as involved as possible. The right equipment is crucial."

"Yes, boss."

Another lusty, turquoise glare. "I'll boss *you*, honey. Don't even get me started."

I feel the heat rise to my face but…I can't help it. I want to push him, because I *know* why he's so grumpy. He's big and male and gorgeous…*and very, very hard.* The ridge inside his jeans is so enormous it looks like someone stuffed a giant kielbasa down there.

Yikes.

It's intimidating but at the same time…I want to tease him. There's something empowering and *fun* about having him entirely at my mercy. Because I'm not scared of him. I *believe* him. I believe all the things he said to me. My question comes out breathily, "How?"

He cocks his head, challenging me with his devil-blue eyes. "You want to know how." His muscles are clenched and he looks almost dangerous. In a good way.

I shrug, sort of coyly. Which isn't like me at all. But… *I love him. And I want him. He's so damn sexy. I don't care about the bet anymore. Didn't he say something about it being one-sided?*

His voice has a rasped edge. "Well, I'll start with your sassy little mouth. I'll kiss you and devour you until you're all hot and *very* wet. I'll peel off all your clothes and I'll bite your ripe little nipples until you squeal. But I won't relent. I'll hold you down and torture you, sucking on you, taking my time, until you're *almost* coming. Then—and this is where I'll be absolutely relentless—I'll kiss my way down to your sweet pussy, eating you with my greedy mouth until you're coming with my tongue inside you. I'm fucking *voracious*, baby. And with every peak of your orgasm, I'll play your clit to make the pleasure last longer, so you'll come even harder. I'll get you nice and wet and ready for me to fuck you with my big, bursting cock. In every position. Until there's no part of you I haven't tasted and possessed as much as I fucking want."

Gage meets my shock with a self-satisfied, wolfish grin. Then he leans closer, murmuring into my ear. "You like my dirty mouth, don't you, baby?" He nips my earlobe. "You *love* how hard I am for you. You want to touch my big cock and feel how hot and hard I am for you, I can see that. I bet you're already wet for me. I bet if I slid my fingers inside your panties right now, you'd be all soft and wet and juicy like the sweetest fruit in the world, isn't that right? You're just aching for me to eat you real good and make you come, aren't you, Luna?"

God.

Yes.

"And I'm going to find out exactly *how* wet you are for me very soon. But first you're going to open these."

It take me a second to regain my composure. I *am* wet.

Very wet. My panties and my tight shorts are clinging to me. And my heart is beating fast.

Relaxed and smug as hell, he hands me the wrapped package.

Not at all recovered, I rip the paper off. It's a brand new MacBook Pro, an iPhone and an iPad, all the newest models. "Gage. This is too much." It's true my old iPhone 6 doesn't have enough storage to download any new apps, or even take more photos. I haven't had a chance to buy more cloud storage.

"You'll need those to keep in touch with Josie more reliably and also to communicate with the contractors, builders and designers. These devices are fully loaded with all the software you'll need, including the architecture and design programs, so you can work with them to create the exact look you want. The teams arrive at ten a.m. on Thursday. Some of them are flying in from around the country."

"Teams?"

"Yes. Now open the envelope."

I do, and slide out a stack of papers. "What is this?"

"I spoke to the bank manager yesterday. Actually, he's the CEO."

"On a Sunday?"

"Yes." He's Gage McCabe, I remember. Investment prodigy and money-making genius. Of course they'll talk to him on a Sunday. "We're changing the name, by the way." His arrogance is back, in full force.

"You changed it without even *asking* me? Why would you do that?" Damn him and his 51%! "What did you change it to?"

"Luna's."

I don't know whether to be furious or absolutely touched. "Luna's?"

"Yes. Read it out loud."

Not entirely forgiving him, I start reading. "'This title confirms that Luna C. LaRoux is the rightful owner and shareholder of ninety-nine percent of *Luna's*, formerly the *Sea Breeze*, including real estate, buildings, outbuildings, fittings and chattels, with one percent retained by Gage McCabe of McCabe Enterprises...'" I stop reading. "Gage. I don't—"

"I retained one percent so I can invest in the business without having to gift it. It's easier."

"But...I can't afford to pay you out. Or take on that big of a mortgage."

"There's no mortgage. I bought it. It's yours. I meant everything I said, honey. That bet was a terrible idea, by the way. I had to make sure you have no reason to keep any distance from me whatsoever."

I can't believe what he's telling me. "You bought the whole thing?"

"Yes. For you. And there are two more contracts there. Read the next one."

I leaf through to the next bundle of papers. But it's blurry. My eyes are pooling with tears. "I can't."

Gage takes the papers and sets them aside. He lifts me onto his lap. *Oh God. His cock is literally gigantic and as hard as granite.* "I'll tell you what they say, then. You know the four-star hotel next door, with the jet ski dock?"

"Yes."

"You own that too. We're going to turn it into a five-star resort, with an infinity pool, a large patio and a full spa. It'll be connected to the restaurant, so customers can make a getaway out of it. And the yacht will be available for parties and events. A glass-bottomed boat will take clients out to the yacht, which we have permission to moor off shore. I also bought a slot at the marina for it."

"You did?"

"I did. I had to do *something* to stop myself from breaking down your door all weekend. So I kept myself busy. The third contract is for the building on the other side of the hotel, the one that stands alone and has its own small sandy beach. You know the one?"

"I love that building. It has those two palm trees framing the front windows. I've always wondered what the view would look like from inside."

"Well, you're about to find out. Because it's also yours. It's three stories, currently divided into six apartments and a roof patio. We can live there, sometimes, when we're not traveling and doing all the other things you want to do."

"We're living together?" *Is this really happening? Is it too fast?*

"Yes. And no, it's not too fast. You're going to take me on. You're going to let me try and I'm going to get you to fall in love with me."

I am?

I am. I am going to let him do that. *I think he might already be doing it. I think he's done it already. In that closet.*

"We'll have a manager running the day-to-day operations of the businesses. The contractors will consolidate the residence as you specify. That's what the design and architecture apps will help with. I've got one of the top designers in Chicago coming in to work with us. He's a friend of mine and he's the best in the business. And we'll renovate this space into a larger yoga studio for you, if you'd like to."

"We will?"

"You can run classes or just use it as a retreat. Whatever you want to do."

It's too much. His words—the beautiful ones and the dirty ones—and now this. "Why did you do all this?" I whisper.

"I told you why. To make you happy."

I reach up to touch his face. The stubble of his beard is rough. I let my fingertips skim the sculpted line of his jaw.

"Do you like your presents?" Hopefully. Like maybe there was a possibility that I wouldn't. His arrogance retreats and his expression is almost dazed. "I love your face. You're like a little wood nymph from a magical forest. And the curl of your hair is so sweet. And the color of your eyes, how they change depending on how mad you are at me. I love everything. I couldn't have dreamed you up, sweet Luna."

This is going to require risk, of course, the kind of risk that can make or break a person. But to hell with that. What *isn't* a risk? *This is a risk you've been putting off for five damn years over an innocent mistake*, I fully realize in this moment. *It's a risk you're going to grab with both hands and run with.* "I love the presents, Gage. Of course I do. Thank you."

"I want to give you everything. For you, I want to be the best version of myself."

"You don't need to be anything you're not. And you really didn't need to do all this."

"I did need to."

"So I guess…all bets are off now."

"All bets are way, way off, sugar pie."

My phone, which is somewhere inside my comforter, rings. I fish it out. "Hello?"

"Hi, I'm your Uber. I've sent you four messages. I'm waiting outside."

"Oh. Yeah, thanks…but I'm not going to need that ride. My plans have changed."

"Right. Well, I'm going to have to charge you the cancelation fee."

"Oh. Sure. Sorry to take up your time like that—"

Gage takes the phone out of my hand and ends the call.

His warm hand eases over the nape of my neck, under my hair, and he kisses me. His mouth is hungry, catching succulently at mine. His tongue sinks into my mouth and a low sound escapes him, like he's overcome. "Don't ever be scared of me." His rasped voice is low and sexy. "I'm going to do everything and we're going to take each other to the fucking stars and it's going to be the best thing that's ever happened to either one of us. Don't hold back from me. Give me everything."

"Okay."

His eyes are deep and dark with his need. "I'm going to have to find out how wet you are for me now, baby. I can't fucking take this anymore."

He peels the comforter from around me and sees that I'm dressed in my yoga outfit. There's not much to it, just a pair of tight little shorts and a fitted bralette.

I hear a strangled-sounding sigh that's almost a groan. He's staring at my clothes, or lack thereof.

I look down at myself. "What?"

"You're wearing your yoga outfit."

"Yes. And?"

"I'm going to come around twelve times before I calm down, honey. I'm so fucking hot for you, you're just going to have to get used to me losing my goddamn mind every five seconds."

Gage lifts me up and carries me to my bed.

He lays me back and kisses me again, more deeply this time, holding himself over me. There's a blend of contradictions about him. The over-confident swagger that's wild and almost dazed with desire. The big, wide-shouldered, perfectly proportioned physique that's, despite all his fierce strength, somehow completely at my mercy. His dark hair with its gold effects from the dawn light is messed up from his obsession. *For me.* And I suddenly feel a transformation take hold. *The Gage effect,* I'm calling it. I trust him. And I want him more than I've ever wanted anything, more than safety or assurances.

I'm shamelessly wet for him. My panties feel saturated. As he kisses me in a lush, slow frenzy, I suck on his tongue.

He groans. "I'm about to come already, baby."

His hand holds my face, his thumb brushing against my lower lip as his tongue delves into me, probing and stroking against mine. *The taste of him,* like an alluring, exotic drug. His kisses are lewd and greedy as hell and I know this is how he'll make love to me. Relentlessly, taking everything. He kisses me until I'm simmering with heat and weak with lust. Until I'll give him absolutely anything he wants. He lays himself over me, letting me feel the hard textures of his desire, pressing his stunningly-rigid erection against my flushed, squirming body.

Gage kisses his way down my neck, biting gently, licking with his tongue. I know he'll leave marks. He's rough, I'm learning, but also tender. Those contradictions again, so I never know quite what to expect. He's reading me. Every sigh, every quiver.

His thumb brushes over my nipple through the thin film of my bralette. He squeezes and tugs until I moan. Then he roughly pulls the fabric up, releasing my breasts, which feel full and warm and sensitive. He pulls the fabric up to my wrists, where he binds me, hooking the tightened tie to a curved wooden detail of the bedhead. My hands are tied.

His big, warm hands squeeze and cradle my breasts, nuzzling the coarse surface of his beard against my soft skin.

"You are so fucking *beautiful*," he murmurs.

His tongue flicks against the underside of my nipple, playing it lightly, and I arch up to him. His hungry mouth eases over the budded peak, sucking strongly, biting, twirling with his tongue. He feasts on my breasts, one then the other, like he's drinking some kind of spiritual sustenance from my body. Each rough tug deepens the sweet ache in my nipples, shooting deep channels of warmth to my core. With each pull of his mouth, my clit throbs lightly. If he keeps doing this, I'll come, just like this.

He's impatient. He licks his way down my stomach lustily, licking and gripping me with his strong hands. I can feel the warmth of his heavy breath as he kisses my stomach. It's ticklish and I giggle and squirm. He holds me down, doing exactly what he wants. His tongue dips into my belly button and I laugh and writhe in protest as a fresh wave of wetness coats my pussy. I can feel his smile against my skin.

He licks his way to the top edge of my shorts, grabbing it with his teeth, pulling my shorts lower. As he does this his fingers skim, finding the wet spot. "Damn, baby, you're wet as fuck. You want me so bad, don't you, sweet girl? You want my big cock to slide all the way inside and make you come hard, I know you do. Now let me see you. Let me taste nirvana before I lose my fucking mind."

He yanks my shorts and my panties off, peeling them down my legs and tossing them aside.

"*Holy fuck*," he groans, when he sees that I'm completely bare. I decided to start waxing a while ago. I do a lot of yoga and get sweaty and it just felt better so I kept doing it. He pulls my legs wider, positioning himself between them, nuzzling me and kissing my skin. "*Mine.* And now I'm going to eat this perfect little wet pink pussy until you come hard. Are you ready for me?"

Oh, God. Am I?

"Wrap your legs around my shoulders. That's it. Now say, 'Eat me, Gage. Make me come, fuck me hard with that big cock.' Say it."

"*Please, Gage.*"

I moan as Gage's tongue bathes my pussy with warm, wet, ruthless strokes. He licks my clit slowly, swirling it with his tongue as he slides two fingers into me, rubbing an excruciatingly sensitive place inside me. I sob with pleasure. It's too good. He continues his languid rhythm and I move with him, writhing against his greedy mouth. He eats into me, licking and sucking hungrily. He's *dirty*. And so, so good at this. His fingers stroke my inner softness as his mouth fastens over my clit. I twist because the pleasure is crazy. He stays with me and I moan his name as he suckles my taut bud, using his tongue and his mouth and his fingers relentlessly until the rapture climbs to a rushing swell that's more than I can handle. Arched against his mouth, I cry out. He nurses the pleasure, sucking harder and rubbing faster as my inner muscles spasm in voluptuous bursts that squeeze and saturate his sticky fingers.

Gage's mouth gentles but he continues to eat at me, like he's addicted. Like he'll never be able to get enough. I can't move. I'm dazed by a physical euphoria that's drugging. It's sort of mind-blowing how outrageously intimate this is. His mouth and his tongue explore and suckle, his rough beard heightening the pleasure-pain as he tenderly coaxes another wave of bliss. And another.

Time takes on an otherworldly feel. I lose count of the orgasms. Six, maybe.

Then he climbs up my body, swiping his forearm across his wet mouth lasciviously, pulling off his shirt, which dishevels his hair even more. *Wow.* His powerful chest is dusted with dark hair. His olive skin looks dark in the morning light. He straddles me, holding me down. He releases my hands, untying me, and I reach out to touch my fingers to his eight-pack, fascinated by the smooth, quilted perfection of his muscles.

An understanding shimmers in the pale inflections of his eyes. They're extraordinary eyes. Dark-rimmed and lightning-bright.

He's checking, I realize. To make sure I'm not scared.

I'll never hurt you.

I know he won't hurt me. I almost *want* him to hurt me, because the pain Gage gives is all about intense, stunning pleasure.

I lay quietly, my pussy still fluttering with ripples of lingering pleasure.

"Are you ready for more, baby girl?"

I'll be careful with you. I want to make you happy.

"I'm ready for everything."

Something wild and restless is taking place between us. Wild lust with a deeper edge.

I love him. And he loves me.

It's so unlikely, so sudden.

So real.

I want to follow it and see where it leads. I want him to infuse me with his glory.

As he leans closer, my hands slide over the nape of his neck. Into that thick black hair. I pull him down to me so his face is close to mine.

"I want you so damn much," he murmurs, staring into my eyes.

Reaching up to him, I kiss his mouth in a seductive

claim. I arch closer and our bodies meet in tantalizing harmony. Rigid, uncompromising hardness over supple, inviting softness.

Gage supports his weight as he unbuttons his jeans. He reaches into his pocket and pulls out a condom packet.

"I'm on the pill," I tell him, "but put it on if you want."

His gaze is searching.

"You don't make that mistake twice," I whisper. How empowering it is to *talk*, even in whispers, about what now feels like an entirely different lifetime.

"I've never done it without holstering the gun." He considers this for a milli-second. Then he kicks off his jeans. "But hell yes, baby, if you'll have me bareback then that's what you're going to get. I'm going to fill you up with my hot seed until you're fucking swimming in it."

I gasp, as I get my very first glimpse at his…*Jesus*. His cock is freaking *colossal*. Long and thick, stunningly hard, dusky and taut against his arrow line of hair—*all the way up his stomach*—with a glimmer of moisture at the broad tip. It's hot-looking with ridges of smooth veins. He's not only ridiculously well-hung he's also very, *very* aroused.

I lace my hand over my mouth and I can't stop a burst of laughter from escaping as my head falls back on the pillow.

He lays his big, playful, fever-hot body over mine.

"I'm not sure what to say when your first reaction is laughter."

This makes me laugh even more. "It's *huge*."

Gage's smile turns hot as he holds his massive cock in his fist. "Yes," he murmurs darkly. "And it wants to fuck that perfect little juicy-as-fuck pussy until you're tugging the cum out of me in hot gushes."

Oh, God.

He touches the head of his cock to my still-pulsing pussy. He rubs the warm, broad crown with its seeping bead of moisture over my clit, which is so sensitive from the six orgasms he's already given me, I feel the pleasure rushes starting again. What I'm learning is that Gage McCabe is outstandingly gifted. And that his *endowments to die for* are exactly that. It's a hot, thick magic wand and he knows exactly how to use it. He swirls the head against my hyper-sensitive nub, teasing the pleasure higher. As he feels the throb of my orgasm starting, he eases the head of his cock inside me. I'm too tight, but so slippery from his mouth and my own honey, he slides further inside me. He uses the wetness to force his way deeper. And deeper. It's too much. The stretching burn of his enormous cock sliding thickly into me pushes me over another precipice of unendurable pleasure. My pussy clenches tightly around his bulk in a furtive rhythm.

Gage groans an agonized hum. "*Hell, I can't hold this. Luna. Luna. You're heaven on earth. Oh, fuck.*"

Gage comes hard, his breath hissing between his clenched teeth as his cock bucks violently inside me, flooding me with heat and triggering another starry wave of pleasure.

He rides my bliss in deep, crazy sync as we come together.

It lasts a long time. There's something beyond physical about the *need* our bodies have for each other's. We're wetly, tightly bound. We're still coming. We're sweaty and entwined. He kisses me and my hands weave through his hair. He stares deep into my eyes as he thrusts again, triggering new tremors of rapture. I can feel the throb of him deep inside me as his cock pulses with the last gushes of his release.

Gage doesn't pull out. He kisses me for a long time, feasting on my mouth and my breasts until his big cock is fully revived, until we're doing it all over again, until he's spilling more of his hot cum deep inside me.

Until it's late afternoon and we're still in bed.

"That proves I was right," he says softly, playing with my hair.

"About what?"

"We're perfect for each other. I knew it the minute I saw you, it happened that fast."

I wrap my legs more tightly around him so his cock slides even deeper. "Maybe you're right."

He smiles. *The* smile. His wolfish smile with an almost-vulnerable edge to it that makes me realize: *I'm his weak-ness.* I'm his one vulnerability. "You're mine," he whispers. "I found you. And now that I have, I'm never letting go."

GAGE PICKS me up and carries me into the shower. He could lift twelve of me without breaking a sweat. I wrap my arms and legs around him. I don't know what day it is, only that it's evening now. The sun is starting to set outside the small etched window in my shower. He kisses me, plunging his tongue into my mouth, exploring intimate angles. There's an edge to him, a desperation. His need has deepened into a barely-controlled frenzy. The more he gets, the more he wants. His mouth is greedy. He takes my mouth almost savagely. Water sluices across our skin, running in tickling rivulets. He grips my thighs hard, murmuring to me between long, lush kisses.

I'm fucking crazy for you. I need to be inside you right now. I need to fucking stay inside you and live inside you. I need to fuck you hard and make you come for me. Only me.

Gage leans me up against the tiled wall. The heavy bulk of him is as hot as newly-forged steel and just as hard. He slides his fingers across my slippery pussy, positioning the head of his cock between my intimate folds, forcing his way inside.

You're so fucking tight, baby. So perfect. Let me in. That's my girl. Fuck, I love how you feel. You're an angel. You're a goddess. You're a fucking dream. That's it, let me in. Squeeze me, come for me. Oh, fuck, you're too beautiful.

The insane thickness of him as he plunges deep stretches me, opening me. I'm so tight around him I can feel the ridges of veins as he drives harder. The burn is painful, star-studded with shards of hot, explosive pleasure. It's like he's made of pure magic. His cock, so big and so deep, rubs rhythmically against every trigger I possess, igniting shattering bursts of rapture as he thrusts into me, over and over.

I grip onto him, struggling to cope with the overload. I come in jolting bursts, each wet compression drawing him deeper, and deeper, until his massive arousal is fully rooted. It's too much. I cry out as the stretching totality of his slick depth tips me over another crazy cliff. I come again, *very, very hard.* My inner muscles pull and tug, milking him with soft, clamping adoration.

Gage growls my name as his cock bucks forcefully inside me, lifting me with burst after burst of his thick, flooding warmth.

He holds me against his big frame as the water rains down on us and our breathing starts to slow.

We stare at each other through the mist, coming to terms with the connectivity of what's taking place here. It's heavy. Like we've jumped in at some ridiculously-uninhibited deep end and we're only swimming deeper.

"Did I hurt you?" His voice is deep and raw with emotion.

"No, Gage."

"I get carried away with you. I'm a beast and a bastard."

I smile against his lips. I used to think of him that way. "You didn't hurt me."

"I was rough with you."

"I like you rough." With the tiniest emphasis on the *you.* I say it carefully. "I think you just fixed me. I think you just replaced everything I was once scared of with your crazy beauty." He has. Just like that.

"I love you," he whispers.

Gage's eyelashes are black and spiked from the water that drips from his hair. As I stare into those eyes, every cell in my body sort of calms and melts with a vast, effortless craving. He's changing me, with his powerful body and his fierce desire. I want to let him in. I want to be with him and explore all the complexities of who he is. I want to give him everything.

I don't know what's happening. Or why. All I know is

that something *is* happening. A shift. A curling, rambling bond is taking hold that's more profound than anything that's ever happened to me. And I can recognize it for what it is.

A star-crossed lucky score.

Love.

EPILOGUE #1

As it turns out, Gage never did leave. We ordered food to be sent up from the restaurant and we stayed in bed for the whole week. We made love so much I could barely walk but I have never felt so beautiful and content and hopeful.

All it took was a stampede, a whiskey-assisted therapy session on a night-lit beach, a heartfelt confession and, finally, several very intense days in bed with Gage McCabe, on the receiving end of his substantial *gifts*—to put it mildly—to fall head over heels in love with him. I was slightly miffed by how smug he was about the fact that it happened so fast, but there was no point fighting him. Fighting only gets us even hotter for each other.

I became a prodigy under his influence, he said. I simply can't get enough of him.

Orgasms change a person. Orgasms given by a

certain well-hung investment guru *transform* a person. It's empowering. I crave him with everything I have. I want to drink him in and taste him and take him inside every chance I get.

To say he feels the same way would be an understatement.

The builders and designers and architects arrived and it has been a whirlwind of activity. My apartment has become our headquarters. Gage sits with me in the meetings but leaves all the decision-making to me. Whatever I want, he says. Whatever makes me happy.

All three buildings are basically being gutted, keeping every ounce of character but refitting everything that isn't either structural or in keeping with the design vision. The decks, the pools and the exterior spaces are all being redone. The interiors are being transformed into stylish, understated Key West décor with a modern, tropical flair. The designer, Gage's friend from Chicago, is turning out to be a genius. His name is Felix and he comes up with ideas I never would have thought of, which I suppose is his job, but he's incredibly good at it.

We've closed the restaurant for six weeks while the refurbishments are being completed. I gave all my staff a paid, much-needed vacation. We're planning to re-open on New Year's Eve. The Tucker Brothers Band will play at the grand opening of *Luna's*.

Gage took me to New Orleans for a week. We walked the streets hand in hand, listened to music, ate amazing food, went shopping, took a ride on a Mississippi river-boat and spent a lot of time in our swanky hotel room.

Gage takes me to a place of physical enlightenment that I think must be, in itself, a rare gift. There's nothing he won't do. He's dirty as hell (in the best kind of way), exceptionally thorough and absolutely relentless. From that first confession, he tells me he loves me a hundred times a day.

On our last night in New Orleans, I said it back to him. My sweet, beautiful, arrogant bastard cried when I said it. We both cried. Then we laughed because his reply was, *I don't blame you. It would be hard not to love all this.*

I talk to Josie every day and she's settled into her routines in Iowa easily enough. She's living in Owen's main house while he renovates and lives in his barn. She's been in touch with Noah every day since she got back and they talk for hours, sometimes late into the night. He's planning to visit her the week before Christmas.

Gage invited me to spend Christmas with him, his brothers and his cousins. So it turns out we'll be spending two days with the Tuckers in Nashville.

He took me to Chicago for a weekend, to see his penthouse apartment, his offices and his life. His former life, as he puts it. As soon as we got there, actual paparazzi were swarming around us, taking pictures. I hadn't realized how famous he was in his hometown. And how much the people there—especially women—compete for his attention. Gage kept his arm around me the entire time. He wouldn't let go of my hand. He kissed me in front of the crowds. If anything, he seemed *more* obsessed and crazed than usual while we were in Chicago, which I wasn't quite expecting. If I needed proof that he loves me, he gave it to me that weekend in spades. Not that I really did. It's another gift he's given me: I *believe* him.

He'll keep the apartment in Chicago available for us and run his companies remotely from Key West. It's not that I didn't like Chicago—I did, and it'll be a fun place to spend time with him—but I'd miss the warm humidity and the Key West flavor in the air. The sand and the sun and the way my heart lifts as soon as I drive across the Seven Mile Bridge.

Gage says wherever I am is his home now.

With us, it got very intense very quickly, but there didn't seem to be any reason to try to slow it down. We've been inseparable since the morning he broke into my apartment to confess his love for me. We only seem to get more addicted to each other with each passing hour.

He insists that we're going to spend a month next summer at his lake house in Michigan. He has several but one of them is his favorite place in the world, he said. I'm excited to see it, and to spend time with him there.

My tiny, rustic apartment will stay mostly the same and will be the last thing to be renovated, once our new house is ready for us to move into. It'll be turned into a cute and slightly more modern yoga studio and I've decided to teach a few classes when we reopen.

For now, I still do my practice each day. I have a new student. Or at least a very enthusiastic observer. He's terrible at yoga. Mostly because he won't concentrate.

"Stop that," I tell him. "You're distracting me."

"You're distracting *me*."

This happens all the time.

I'm in child's pose and he's kneeling behind me, off his mat. "Get back on your mat," I say.

"I like your mat better."

He's dressed in only a pair of shorts that aren't even yoga shorts.

His hand slides over my back, massaging me gently. Then it glides lower, over my hips and between my legs, where he cups me with his warm palm. His fingers play and he gently massages my clit. Until I can feel the warmth. "Just as I thought. You're getting wet for me. And I can't have that go unattended."

I gasp lightly as he lazily squeezes and rubs me intimately until my panties and shorts are wet to the touch.

"Let's get tantric," he murmurs lecherously.

"That's *all* you want to do, is get tantric. What about yoga?"

"I can't do yoga like *this*." I turn to look at what he means, even though I already know. His cock is fully hard and halfway out of his shorts, glistening with moisture.

I laugh, exasperated, because…no, he really *can't* do yoga like this. And he looks too delicious for *me* to be able to do yoga with him like this. I crawl closer. "Lay back," I say gently, guiding him onto the mat so he's lying flat on his back. He rests his head on a bent, burly arm. I kneel over him, running my hands over his hair-dusted chest, loving the feel and appreciating the sublime shape of his big, sculpted body. He lets me explore, watching me as I unzip his shorts, fully revealing him to me.

I grip his engorged shaft with both hands and lift it away from his stomach. Slowly, I lick the moisture, sliding my tongue across the slit, taking the head of his cock into my mouth. There's no way I can take all of him, he's far too big, but I grip his thick cock in my fist and suck him deeper. A gush of pre-cum spills onto my tongue.

"*Luna*," he growls. "*Fuck.*"

I find an awkward rhythm, sucking on him as tenderly as I can, drawing him further and further into my mouth, using my tongue and my hands to stroke him.

It doesn't take long. Gage lets out a groan as his cock jerks. Hot liquid jets into my throat, flooding my mouth with his milky seed. I swallow as much as I can, suckling gently on his softening shaft until I've taken all of his essence.

It takes him a few minutes to recover. His eyes are bloodshot as he weaves his fingers through my hair. "Have I told you yet today how much I love you?" he asks huskily.

I smile and think about it for a few seconds. "Twenty-two times."

"I like *this* kind of yoga." He sits up and peels off my

top, then proceeding to pull off my shorts and panties. "My turn." He grabs a towel and lays it over my yoga mat. Then he takes a small bottle of massage oil and unscrews the top. He helps me into position, so I'm lying on my stomach on top of the towel.

He uses the oil to massage my back, rubbing the tension from my muscles.

"Oh, that feels so good."

He massages my shoulders, my arms, then he moves to my legs, getting me completely covered in oil. Moving my legs wider, his fingers glide intimately over my pussy. *Everywhere.* Until I'm warm and wet and slippery.

Gage lifts my hips so I'm on my knees with my knees apart and my head resting on the towel. I arch back, giving him everything he wants. From behind, he licks my pussy in long strokes, pushing his tongue greedily into me. He licks me everywhere, pressing his tongue into every secret cove. Then he draws on my clit with his mouth, nursing gently.

The pleasure from his mouth takes me to a high brink. I'm *so* close. He pulls away and I feel his thick, fully-revived cock sliding into me, stretching me fully to receive his massive length, thrusting deep. The heavy invasion does what it always does. It tips me into a lush orgasm that squeezes and grips him until he groans and comes again in throbbing surges, pumping me full of his seedy liquid heat.

When the last spasms of his release calm, Gage rolls

us to our sides, spooning me and cradling me in his arms, his big bulk still wetly insinuated deep inside me.

"Thank you for healing me," I whisper. "And enlightening me."

He holds me close, kissing my face as he whispers the words. "Thank you for saving me. Thank you for *existing* and giving me a reason to live. You're *beautiful*. You kill me with your sweet perfection. I love you to the moon and back, my Luna. You're the one."

GAGE

It's a strange thing, that you can live a life for twenty-seven years and not feel anything. And that you can then wake up the very next day and suddenly feel *everything.* On fucking steroids. I never thought I would turn into my father but that's basically what's happened, overnight. Except I think I'm even worse. I'll give her the world and I'll kill anyone who touches her. I don't remember my father being the jealous type. He was too distracted by his crazy projects and his own thoughts.

For me, though, half of me is a walking cliché straight out of a cheesy romcom, buying flowers and secretly shopping for wildly expensive diamond rings, and the other half might as well be a digitally-enhanced Spartan with only one thing on his mind: protecting his woman to the death.

I take her to Nashville and they laugh at me. My new

nickname is Caveman. Because if any of my cousins so much as glance in Luna's direction I eyeball them with murder in my eyes.

We have a good time, other than that. Both my brothers' girlfriends are beautiful people. Millie is quiet and sort of ethereal and Bo, hopeless romantic that he is, finally seems comfortable in his own skin. And no wonder. That promise he made to our mother was something I never could have done. I thought he was a sucker for having *that* much integrity. But now I think differently. Now I think of everything differently, like I'm seeing the world and all the people in it from a fresh perspective. *The Luna effect*, I call it.

The outcome of which is that instead of being a total prick all the time, I'm a much better person. I have to say, it feels good.

Caleb's girlfriend Violet is perfect for him. He's a lot calmer than he was last time I saw him. His eyes don't look quite so spooked and he even laughs again. She's easing him out of his dark place, healing him right before our eyes.

I guess that's what love is, and what it does. As the saying goes, it's the cracks that let the light in.

Snow has started lightly falling outside the wall of windows. It's after dinner and we're all sitting around the large game room in Travis's house, with its leather furniture and bar and pool table. There's a fire in the fireplace and the music is turned up. Kade and Violet are playing pool against Millie and Vaughn. Roxie and Luna are standing by the old-style juke box, picking out songs.

I walk over to where Caleb and Bo are sitting in leather chairs by the fire.

We clink glasses.

"She's good for you, Gage," says Bo.

I glance over at her. She's the most gorgeous creature I've ever seen. Every time I look at her she takes my breath away. "Yeah. She is."

Caleb actually grins. "Who would have thought it would happen to all three of us? Just like it happened to them."

We raise our glasses and toast to our parents' memory.

"I just want to know when it's going to happen to *me*," Travis says, joining our circle. He elbows me.

The song ends and I pull the small blue box out of my pocket.

"I have a question I need to ask a certain someone," I say, to the room.

They all turn and look at me.

I walk over to where Luna is standing there in her jeans and her yellow sweater with her eyes that look gold in the warm light and her face like a dream. Better than a dream. Because she's real and she's mine. "It's Christmas Eve so I thought it might be a good time to do this even though I've been wanting to do it for a while now but I wasn't sure if she was ready. And I sure as hell hope she's ready now."

Everyone gets very quiet.

Luna stares at me with wide eyes as I get down onto one knee and open the small box I'm holding.

I take a deep breath. "Luna. I love you. I want to spend the rest of my life with you because when you know for sure that something is real and too good to be true you want to hold onto it as hard as you can. I want to wake up next to you every morning. I want to give you everything you've ever dreamed of. I love you so much. Luna, will you marry me? Please say yes."

There's a glint of something that might be light but exuberant exasperation. I'm putting her on the spot in front of all these people. I'm forcing her hand, almost, like I've done before. And for a fleeting second, my heart skips a beat because *what if she says no?*

I'll die. I'll chase after her. I'll—

"Yes." She's smiling at me and *I am so in love with her.*

I take her hand and slide the ring onto her finger. Then I stand and pick her up and twirl her around slowly as she kisses me.

Everyone cheers.

A champagne bottle pops.

But the only thing I'm aware of is the taste of her lips and the beauty of this moment and this stunning, perfect girl.

She said yes.

Five years later...

THE GRAND OPENING of *Luna's* was a magical night. Gage hired an army of security and the Tucker Brothers Band played under a full moon on New Year's Eve. We danced and laughed and sang along.

Since then, the businesses have been going exceptionally well. The hotel and spa are booked months in advance and the restaurant is packed every night. We have a full events calendar and the yacht has been a popular party venue.

The house is more than I could have dreamed of. It has huge double-glazed windows rimmed with steel, Dade pine ceilings and lots of open, light-filled, airy spaces. It's decorated with colorful art and leafy, tropical plants. I absolutely adore it.

Gage and I got married at his summer "cottage" on the beach on Lake Michigan. It's a beautiful place and I've fallen in love with it. It's a rambling old house with modern updates. It has views from every window, a dock and we even have a fishing boat. We spend weeks at a time there and it has become our second home.

We've started a tradition with Bo and Millie and Caleb and Violet to spend Christmases there with our growing families. Even Gage, who hates the holidays, is starting to get into the spirit of our festive get-togethers.

Josie and Noah and their children come out and stay with us for long weekends, either at the lake or in Key West. Their one night stand ended up creating a beautiful, thriving family. They've had two more babies, girls this time. Also twins. They live in Big Sur, in the house Noah designed, with views of the ocean. Funny how things work out sometimes.

For our honeymoon, Gage took me to Europe for a month. We went to London, Paris, Rome, Venice and spent a week at a villa in Tuscany. We ate good food, visited the sights and museums, and spent lazy afternoons in bed. Our lovemaking has a beauty and a bond that awes me. I can no longer imagine a life without my husband. I love him more than I knew I *could* love. He's a part of me that feels as real and as important as my own body and soul.

It's a beautiful thing, to love like we do. We don't take it for granted. We treat it like the treasure it is.

I went off the pill just before our honeymoon and I was pregnant by the time we got home.

I cried, for all the right reasons. For the past and most of all for the future.

Gage has stayed true to his word. He's careful with me when I need him to be. His love for me takes away my fears and doesn't leave room for sadness. With him, I'm too *happy* for sadness. Just like he promised.

Our baby girl's name is Isla. She has dark blond hair and turquoise eyes, exactly the same color as her daddy's. Her hair has a jaunty curl to it that won't straighten no matter what we do to it, just like mine.

Two years later we had our son, Elias. He has black hair and eyes that change color with his moods, from green to aqua, even to gold. He's a gorgeous little boy with the same innate self-assurance as his father, who he follows around like an adoring puppy. But when he's tired, he only wants me.

It's evening and I've just finished a yoga class. I've found that I love teaching. Yoga and meditation can change your life and it's fun and rewarding to watch people experience that. Some of my students have become good friends.

Once everyone has left, I turn off the lights of my studio and lock up. I go downstairs to the busy restaurant. I wave to Rico, who's run off his feet but not like the old days, when it was just us. We have a lot more staff now.

I make my way past the hotel, with its expansive patio

and infinity pool, where people are sitting out enjoying the night.

And I let myself into the house.

Gage has put the children to bed and is waiting for me on the couch, scrolling on his iPad. He looks up when I walk in. His hot gaze rakes over my yoga outfit. "Hey, beautiful. How's my dazzling wife?"

He puts the iPad aside and I sit on his lap. "Happy," I tell him. "You did it. You made all my dreams come true."

"Told you," he says smugly.

I straddle his hips and feel that he's already getting hard for me. "Except…well, I was thinking there might be one more thing I'd like."

"What thing?"

I kiss his lips, licking lightly between them. "I was thinking maybe we could have one more baby."

He lifts me into his arms and carries me upstairs. "One more. Or two more. Maybe three more. You can have whatever you want."

I wrap my arms around his neck. "I love you."

Gage smiles down at me, kicking the door of our bedroom closed behind us. "Of course you do. It would be impossible not to."

We laugh and my beautiful husband takes me to bed.

Thank you so much for reading **Arrogant Player**. I hope you enjoyed Gage and Luna's love story.

Reviews are like gold to authors. They help new readers find our books. If you enjoyed Gage and Luna's story, please consider leaving a quick a review or rating on Amazon.

Below I've included the first chapter of **Hopeless Romantic**, Bo and Millie's story, which is a standalone novella and the first book in the McCabe Brothers series. It's my tribute to love at first sight and insta-everything (because it happened to me :).

I'm also including Chapter One of **Nashville Days.** This is the first book in a sexy spin-off series to the McCabe Brothers series (hot cousins!) called the Music City Lovers series. It's a steamy small town rockstar romance.

xoxo,
Julie Capulet

Please come join my Facebook reader group, Julie Capulet's Romantics, where I share cover reveals, insider info and we discuss all things romance!

Sign up for my newsletter to receive my free bonus content and get access to sneak peeks and exclusive giveaways!

Visit my website @ www.juliecapulet.com

When he falls, he falls *hard*.

Millie Baylin just moved to a new city to start college. Introverted and studious, she plans on spending most of her time holed up in the library working on her novel and keeping to herself. But when she gets dragged along to a school football game by her fun, football-mad new roommate, the hot star quarterback almost drops the ball at his very first sight of her.

Bo McCabe is saving himself. A hopeless romantic at heart, he's holding out for the real thing. As soon as he lays eyes on the shy stranger with the striking gray eyes and the angel's face, he'll stop at nothing to find out if she's the one he's been waiting for all along.

Millie thinks Bo's insta-obsession is insanity and wants nothing to do with him. But Bo is determined. Because, somehow, Millie has already stolen his heart…and he is now utterly obsessed with winning hers.

Can Bo convince Millie he's the man of her dreams?

Hopeless Romantic is a sexy standalone sports romance, starring an obsessed hero and the love of his life (includes three hopelessly romantic HEA epilogues!). This book is a tribute to love at first sight and insta-everything (because it happened to me :).

McCabe Brothers

Chapter One

Millie

The bus drops me next to the front entrance of the university and I walk up to the main admissions building, where I'm given a map and a bag full of booklets and welcome materials. I make my way through the crowd of people on the campus green, keeping my hat low over my eyes, using the map to try to find my way to my new dorm.

I can't believe I'm here.

College.

I never knew if I'd actually get this far. So many times along the way, college had seemed like a place *other* people went, a goal not just up among the stars, but over in someone else's galaxy. But I've made it. This is *real.* My dream, against all odds, has come true.

I graduated from high school more than a year ago, but it's taken me this long to save up enough money to get started. Desperate to get as far away from my hometown in Florida as possible, I applied to four schools. *And I got in.*

This place is like a different world. More than forty thousand students go to this university. It's practically its own city, with top-ranked sports teams, space-age libraries and students from every walk of life you could imagine. It's got an energetic, optimistic vibe to it that's kind of blowing my mind. The autumn air is crisp and cool. People are pink-cheeked, wearing colorful scarves, holding steaming cups of coffee and hot chocolate from a nearby coffee truck. Until two days ago, I'd never in my life been north of Atlanta. Everything about this place feels new and exciting and picture-perfect. I almost feel like I belong here.

Belonging isn't something I've had a lot of experience with. I don't fit in or make friends easily. Not because I intentionally try to be an outcast, but because I'm used to keeping secrets.

But not anymore.

All my secrets have turned to dust.

Here, I'm not the poor kid with a heroin addict for a

mother. Or the lonely waif who lives in a trailer park and carries Narcan in her pockets. I'm not the freaky teenage girl who wears hats and oversized jackets in August to hide myself because I live alone, or close enough. My only protector was too far gone to care.

All that's behind me now.

My mother is dead. It feels like a mercy. The needles, the wasting away, the giving up of every shred of herself just to get her next fix. I tried to save her, but she just couldn't be saved. Grief was weaved into the painful fabric of our downward spiral. Which meant that, as soon as she was gone, it was surprisingly easy to walk away. I'd already said my goodbyes to the person my mother was, a long time ago.

Now, I'm *free*. Free of the pain and sadness of my past.

Today, here—right this minute—I can start my new life.

In this mini-city of forty thousand people, I know I can find my own quiet corner, where I'll be perfectly content to watch everyone else having the time of their lives while I get to work and do what I came here to do. Kick ass, in the only way I know how.

It's a strange thing to have a knack for. As soon as I started writing stories, something clicked. When I write, I enter this fever dream that takes me into other worlds. I use writing to crawl inside my own mind. To escape from reality. It helped, when I needed it most.

The coffee-scented air leads me over to the coffee

truck. I stand in line. I'm wearing my usual loose jacket and my black sailor's cap that I tuck my hair into. Because I actually *need* them in this weather, which is a nice change. People still stare at me. I'm used to it. I know what I look like.

Students are clustered into groups, talking to each other, *meeting* each other. I sometimes wonder, like now, what it would be like to be fun and outgoing. The girl behind me in line starts up bubbly conversations with a couple of random strangers, without even a hint of self-consciousness or turning red or stammering over her words, like I would. Shyness is a curse.

My backstory doesn't help, but at some point, you just have to move on. That's why I'm here, after all.

"What can I get you?" says the guy in the truck. He's staring. I pull my hat a little lower.

"One hot chocolate, please."

He smiles, making no move to get my order. "You must be a freshman. I'm sure I would have noticed you."

"Yes. I just arrived." After three days on a Greyhound bus, but I don't bother with the details.

He pours cocoa into a cardboard cup. "I'm Mason."

"Hi, Mason."

I don't offer my name in return. There's a line behind me and I really just want to get my drink so I can go and find my dorm. But Mason takes his time. "And you are?"

I relent. "Millie."

"Millie," he repeats. "I like that name."

"It's sort of old-fashioned, but it works."

His gaze roves across my face, taking its time. "Hey, there's a party at my place tonight. You should come." He scrawls a number on a napkin and hands it to me, along with my cup of hot chocolate. "Give me a call."

"I'll see. Thanks." I hand him my money card.

"It's on the house," he says. "Really. You should come. It'll be fun. I can pick you up if you need a ride."

"Hey, man," says a guy behind me in line. "How about stop trying to pick up the freshman and make us some coffee instead?"

I take that as my cue. "Thanks, Mason."

"See you tonight, hopefully," Mason calls after me, but I let myself drift into the crowd. I already know I'm not going to Mason's party. I'm not really the party-going type. Besides, I don't have time. Part of being able to afford college came from the advance money for a book I wrote last year, when I was going through the worst of … the worst. By some miracle, I landed a literary agent, who got me a two-book deal with a major publisher. They said my writing was "heartfelt," which is true enough. The money isn't a huge amount, but it meant I could afford to start college this year, instead of waiting another year or two to save. I have no idea how I'll finish the second book by their deadline of January 1st, but I guess I'll figure it out. That, along with the full course load I'll be taking, means I'll basically be living in the library for the entire first semester.

I check my map, pretending I feel confident and ready to take my new world by storm. At least if I *look* like I know what I'm doing, people might actually think I do.

There's a band playing a Fleetwood Mac song in the middle of the green. Nearby, some guys are throwing a football around.

The sky is blue, with only a few high, wispy clouds. It's late afternoon. The leafy trees are vibrant shades of red and orange, with an artful smattering sprinkled across the green grass. Autumn, like I've only seen it in movies. Everything's so colorful and … *collegiate.* Preppies, jocks, hipsters and academics are mingling seamlessly, all wearing splashes of the same school colors.

Nearby, a cluster of girls are eyeing up the football jocks. These are the kinds of girls who used to make my life hell in high school. The social media-obsessed types who spend hours making sure their selfies are envy-worthy. They hate people like me: people with problems they don't want touching them and their shiny lives. Loners, who—God knows why, since I avidly try to avoid it—take attention away from them. And it's always the kind of attention I wish I wasn't getting.

I do my best to avoid them. Maybe things will be different in college.

I'm mortified when one of the jocks calls out to me and starts walking over to me. He's huge and built like a Marvel character.

I try to steer clear but he blocks my way, so I'm forced to stop.

"Hey," he says. He's literally towering over me. I have no doubt he could break me in half if he wanted to. It's intimidating. "Are you a freshman?"

I just had this conversation and I really don't feel like having it again. I'm not good at small talk. "Yes. And I'm on my way to my dorm, if you'll excuse me."

"You're fucking *gorgeous*," he says.

I don't know how to reply to that so I step around him and keep walking but he walks along with me.

He's persistent. "Where're you from?"

I don't want to chit-chat with this oversized stranger. "A small town I'm sure you've never heard of."

"Try me." He's sort of sweaty and bulging and it's freaking me out.

So I hurry past him. "I'm sorry but I'm meeting someone and I'm late. It was nice talking to you."

"You and me should get together sometime," he says.

That's not going to happen in this lifetime or the next twelve, I don't bother saying. I keep walking, hoping I'm heading in the right direction.

"I'll look out for you," the jock calls after me.

Luckily, unless he likes hanging out in hidden corners of the library, he'll never find me.

My dorm isn't far. It's full of people carrying boxes and saying goodbye to their parents. A pang of something that's not quite sadness and not quite jealousy flutters, but

I let it go. It doesn't matter anymore that I'm alone. These people are starting their new lives too, just like I am. Some are already partying. I slide past them and make my way up to the third floor.

My roommate is there, sitting on the bed next to the window that has a view out over the green. She's going through an open suitcase and she looks up when I walk in. She has long hair the color of polished copper and a sprinkling of freckles across her nose. Her face lights up, like she's genuinely happy to see me. "Hey, roomie. I'm Violet."

I smile back at her. It's impossible not to. She's fun and nice, you just get that impression. "Millie."

"Hi, Millie. I hope you don't mind me claiming the bed next to the window. And the bigger closet. Your desk is bigger, though. And you have an extra bookshelf."

"No, that's fine."

"I saw you talking to that football player and his groupies," she says.

"You saw that?"

"I was feeling your pain." She laughs. "Those girls' faces when they saw it was *you* and not them he was chasing after."

"Well, they can have him. I hope I haven't already made a few enemies."

"Those girls will be fine as long as you stay away from the football team."

"You know them?"

"I know their type." She sets a picture of her family on her bedside table. She has a lot of brothers, it looks like. "My brother was the quarterback at my high school in Wilmington. My other brother was a wide receiver. And my *other* brother was a halfback. We had girls like that camping out on our doorstep every night of the week."

"Wow. Well, I'll definitely be staying away from the football team," I assure her. "As far away as possible."

"There's no way we're not going to the game tonight, though. You *have* to come with me. I don't know anyone else here yet."

I laugh a little as I put my bag on my bed and start unpacking it. "I'm probably going to skip the game, sorry."

"No *way*, roomie, you can't bail on me! I refuse to sit there by myself and I can't miss the opening game of the season. My brothers would kill me."

"I'm not really into football," I admit. I've honestly never watched much of it and couldn't tell you the rules if my life depended on it.

"What are you into?" Violet's face is open and sunny, like she's actually interested and not just asking to make small talk. So I find myself telling her.

"I'm a writer."

"That's so cool! Are you an English major?"

"Yeah. How about you?"

"Psychology. I'm planning on becoming a shrink. Believe it or not, it's been my lifelong ambition."

"Wow." I start putting some of my stuff into drawers.

"Yeah, just be careful. I might go all Freudian and start psycho-analyzing you any minute."

I smile without meaning to and it feels good. It's been a long time since I made a new friend. "I'll watch out for that."

"If you ever feel like you might need some therapy, just let me know. You can be my first patient."

I take my hat off and toss it onto my bed. My hair tumbles out and hangs past my shoulders. It's been a while since I cut it.

"Wow," she says. "Is that your real hair?"

I have strange hair. It's a very pale shade of red that's almost blond, but not quite. It looks pink under certain lights. A lot of people comment on it or stare at it or want to touch it, which is why I usually keep it hidden. I cut it shorter after my mother died, in one of those weird moments where you do something and you don't know why. But it's grown back since then. I have bangs and it's angled around my face, unevenly in places, because going to a hairdresser wasn't something I could ever afford. "I'm thinking about dyeing it black."

"Don't you dare. It's amazing."

"So's yours." It really is. It's a coppery red with gold highlights.

Her phone pings and she's busy for a few seconds. "So, what do you say? Kick-off is at four thirty."

"I don't know the first thing about football."

"I'll teach you," she says. "Who knows, you might actually enjoy it."

My HERO

Caleb McCabe just returned from a tour of duty. He's shell-shocked. Loud noises make him jump. He feels like an outcast in civilian society. When Caleb meets a gorgeous, fun-loving redhead named Violet, he knows he can't handle a relationship, especially with a ray of sunshine like her. But that doesn't stop him from thinking about her day and night.

Violet Jameson is studying for a degree in psychology. When she meets the ultra-hot combat hero Caleb, she's riveted not only by his rugged good looks but also by his obvious vulnerabilities. She yearns to get close to him, and to begin to heal him. They share a night of passion that's so hot she realizes she's not only in lust but in love.

For Violet's sake, Caleb tries to stay away. He wants her more than he can bear, but he's afraid of hurting her with his own emotional scars. The problem is, no matter how much he fights his obsession, he can't stop himself. He has to make her his. He knows in his heart she's the one.

Caleb and Violet are meant for each other, but will his dark damages get in the way of their Happily Ever After?

My Hero is a sexy standalone romance starring a battle-scarred alpha hero and the sweet, sassy redhead who changes everything.

McCabe Brothers

Every song he wrote was about a girl he hadn't met yet. Then she walked into his life.

Travis Tucker is a country-rock superstar. With four number one albums, sold-out tours and millions of fans, he's living the dream. But somewhere along the way, the spotlight lost its shine. Travis can never find the one thing he's been writing all his songs about: *real* love. So he decides to buy himself a country getaway to work on his next record and clear his head.

Ruby Hayes is a small town girl with big dreams. Finally free of boarding school, she plans on spending the summer writing songs on the piano in the abandoned farmhouse next door. Then she's on her way to Nashville.

When Travis finds Ruby, singing like an angel at his piano, he falls *hard*. Now that he's finally found the girl he's been searching for, Ruby ignites in him a wild obsession that's hotter than the Tennessee sun. And she has no idea who he is.

For Ruby, things get complicated. With a voice that's somehow familiar, like he's already a part of her, Travis is a temptation she can't resist.

The summer becomes a feverish haze of hot nights, shared lyrics, and the kind of spark that blazes into wildfire.

But summer can't last forever. Can their love survive beyond it, with the demands of Travis's high-profile life, Ruby's ambition and a jealous best friend threatening to come between them?

Or is this a love story written in both the music and the stars?

Nashville Days is a steamy standalone small town rockstar romance starring a hot, hopelessly romantic lead singer and the sweet & sassy songbird who steals his heart. Perfect for fans of Elsie Silver.

Music City Lovers

"I want to thank ya'll for coming out tonight, Austin. You know we love you." The crowd roars.

We play our last song, our newest number one hit. I can barely hear my own voice as a hundred thousand people sing along with me. It's a crazy feeling, having *this* many souls touched by your words and so fully invested, singing their goddamn hearts out. They know every note. They've lived their lives to these lyrics. They've loved, cried and laughed to these tunes. They're filling up the night with their emotion, swaying to the slow rhythm. The lights of their phones shine like a galaxy of stars.

And when we hit that final chord, the thundering cheer of the crowd is deafening. Vaughn climbs down from his drums and the three of us stand there together on stage for a few seconds, taking it all in. The applause of a hundred thousand people is something you don't ever really get used to. The adrenaline rush is just as pure as it was the very first time.

We take a final bow and exit the stage, where a swarm of security surrounds us and ushers us through a bullet-proof corridor toward our tour bus. I can still hear them chanting my name. But we've done our encores after playing for three and a half hours. We're getting close to the end of our 48-show, 38-city tour and I'm feeling it. The highs and lows and the creeping exhaustion that sets in after giving it everything you've got for months on end. We have two final shows left, both at home in Nashville. It's been by far our biggest tour yet.

I feel lit by the crowd, the music, the whiskey and the wine, the satisfaction of pouring my heart and soul into something real. Something that touches people and connects them. Every single show has been sold out. Our record is number one. Four of our songs are in the top ten. And the momentum just keeps on building.

We get to the bus and it's crowded, with groupies and people from the band and hangers-on. Our opening act, Jackson Cole, and his entourage are here, like they always seem to be. The fame and the women are new to him. He's overdosing and finding his feet, maybe. Riding our wave, to a certain extent, but whatever.

Vaughn pours three shots. Roxie gives Kade a hug, then me. She's relieved. Turns out our little sister is a genius at managing us. This tour has been bigger than we ever imagined. Now we can play our last two home shows and finally take a much-needed break before we start another 12-show West Coast tour next month.

I collapse onto one of the plush chairs. I tip back the whiskey Vaughn hands me. One of the groupies puts her hand on my arm and leans close to me. "Travis, you were amazing tonight. You're *so* good."

Do I know her? I don't think so. She might be a new one. It all starts to blur at the edges after a while. They all start looking the same. I'm no saint but I also need to *feel* something before I'll act on the constant stream of attention and adoration I happen to get. Right now I'm not feeling much of anything.

Kade hands me a beer.

"Hell," he says, sitting in the chair next to mine and clinking his bottle against mine. "Texas always has insane crowds. I could hardly even hear us." As usual, Kade's new-ish girlfriend Carmen is hovering around him. Roxie's not a fan. Come to think of it, neither am I. I don't usually care much who my brothers hang out with, but this girl seems to have an effect on Kade that's messing with his head. He's more moody when she's around. Jackson joked that she's our Yoko, waiting in the wings, whispering in his ear all the time about running away together so he can work on his solo album. I don't think that's his plan. Not now, anyway. We're on too much of a roll. And I can't worry about it tonight.

Vaughn laughs and cranks up the music, chugging from the bottle of Jack he's holding. He's got a fat joint in his other hand. A groupie with a lot of piercings and a ridiculously short skirt puts a pink pill on his tongue. Another girl is unbuttoning his shirt. His black hair is unkempt and long. His eyes are bloodshot, which makes them look even more blue than usual.

Roxie pulls one of the girls away from him. "What did you give him?" She pries Vaughn's mouth open but he grins at her, sort of guiltily.

"Too late," he says.

"*Vaughn*," Roxie scolds him. "Booze and weed is one thing. You said no drugs."

"Come on, Rox, I'm celebrating. Give me one night."

"*One* night? You've had three whole *months* of nights."

"I'll go cold turkey after the tour," Vaughn tells her. "I'll take a break."

We've all heard that one before. My brother is out of control, is what it boils down to. And he's only getting worse.

Vaughn has always walked a fine line. Like our father did, until it killed him. Kade and I can easily keep up with our younger brother when it comes to the whiskey—and usually do—most of the time. The difference is, we have downtimes. We lay off when we're not touring. We clean up when we feel like it.

Cleaning up isn't something Vaughn's done in a while. I'm not sure he's even capable of it at this point. Kade and Roxie and I have talked about it. We decided to finish the tour, then we'll sit him down and talk it through with him. Get him some help or check him in somewhere if need be.

None of which is happening tonight.

We're driving all night tonight so we can get back to Nashville in the morning. There's no doubt this party will still be going when we get there.

This bus has been the hub of our non-stop bender all the way through. We all got into a groove of it for the first month or two, but after a while you find yourself getting more and more strung out from the total lack of sleep and peace and quiet. Even before we left, we were hounded like this. We have a loft warehouse we've converted into apartments, a recording studio and an office headquarters in downtown Nashville. We tried to keep the location under wraps but our fans found out about it, like they always do.

"That show was mayhem," says Vaughn. Not that he minds. Mayhem might as well be Vaughn's middle name. As if to confirm this, he blows a couple of smoke rings at me.

Tonight I'm not in the mood to fight my way through crowds of people just so I can go to bed.

What I need is some real sleep. Uninterrupted by banging and knocking and people trying to get in.

I need a quiet place to hang out for a while, I decide. A secret getaway. An old house out in the country somewhere, far from the city and the rabid fans and the never-ending parade of groupies, where there's space and fresh air and days with nothing to do except write. I can't remember the last time I was *alone* for more than a few hours at a time.

I'll find myself someplace off the beaten track, where no one even knows I'm there. I'll sleep and daydream and clear my head. Maybe Vaughn can spend some time there too, and dry out. And Kade, without the girlfriend. All three of us. We'll work on our next record. We'll write our masterpiece, uninterrupted.

I send a message to a real estate agent I sometimes use when I buy new properties. I have three houses: an apartment in Nashville that's part of our headquarters, my own house in Franklin outside Nashville that I need to get a lot more security for because people have set up fucking camps around the peripheral fences, and a condo in L.A. None of them will be either empty or quiet. I have a lot of friends and an open-door policy for the most part, which I'm now starting to severely regret. All my houses have become magnets for hangers-on and their non-stop parties.

I'm looking for another house, I text him. *A farm, maybe, at least a half hour outside Nashville. Something remote. Very private. Surrounded by a lot of land. Maybe with a barn or something I can soundproof and convert into a studio. ASAP.*

Three girls surround me. One of them touches the top button of my shirt. I'm not in the mood to party tonight, go figure. I'm strung out. *Burned* out. I'm twenty-five years old and I already feel like I'm hanging on to the end of a fraying rope. I've been burning the candle at both ends for as long as I can remember and I suddenly feel a new urge for some goddamn solitude.

One of the girls touches my hair. Another whispers in my ear. "You're *so* hot, Travis. I love you so much."

I don't even know her name.

One of the girls weaves her fingers through mine. "We want to show you something in one of the bedrooms, Travis. *All* of us."

My phone pings with a message. It's from my real estate agent. Damn, he's fast. "Maybe later." I don't know, maybe I've become jaded. I don't want to fuck just for the hell of it, not that I ever really did. I'm not an out of control player like Vaughn and I'm not a soulful romantic like Kade. I fall somewhere in the middle. I have a good time without getting serious.

But sometimes—like right now—it occurs to me that I never quite *feel* as much as I wish I did. Never in a way that makes you want to hang on to it or get excited about it or make it last. Never in a way you'd write a goddamn song about. Which is too bad. Because I write a lot of songs. Songs about falling in love and chasing after that one and only true love because you think your heart will break if you can't spend every hour of every day with her until you die.

The truth is, I'm just guessing. Because I've never experienced anything close to that kind of intensity. Which, tonight, feels sort of … sad. All these desperate souls, looking for that one magical, elusive person they can fall in love with to the point that nothing and no one else matters.

Most of them will never find it. *I* might never find it.

Which is sort of tragic when you think about it.

Like now. Women are literally hanging off me. And I feel exactly … nothing. No spark. No interest. Just … boredom. A craving for something *real*.

I stand up and move away, as much as I can in the smoky, noisy, jam-packed space. People are getting loose.

I check the message. *I've got a new listing you might want to see. It's been sitting empty for 4 years and needs some work but it's a premium property. Beaut house. 5 bedrooms. 40 mins east of Nville, remote. Sits on 100 fenced acres with its own pond, a large barn and 3 cabins. Listed at 3.5m. It's bank-owned and available immediately.*

I follow the link and scroll through the photos.

Wow. The place is mint, but he wasn't wrong. It looks dusty and unkempt. In a good way. In a no-one-will-ever-suspect-I'm-there kind of way. I'll leave it like that. I'll become a hermit for the next few weeks and completely tune out. There are pictures of the barn too. It's huge and rustic. And the old cabins, dotted around the property.

The offer is almost too fucking good to be true.

I text him back. *Let me know where to transfer the $. I'll pay cash tonight.*

I'll move in immediately. Hell, I'll drive out there as soon as we get back.

We exchange a few more messages. He confirms that the sale has gone through. He'll have the power turned on. He'll courier the keys so they're there by the time I get to Nashville.

A strange longing settles into me that feels almost like hope. More than that. An eerie sense that something's about to happen …

ALSO BY JULIE CAPULET

I Love You Series

The Obsession Begins (free)

XOXO I Love You

XOXX I Love You More

Love You The Most (free)

Sexy Standalones

Max

Cowboy

McCabe Brothers Series

Hopeless Romantic

My Hero

Arrogant Player

Music City Lovers Series

Nashville Days

Nashville Nights

Nashville Dreams

Nashville Lights

Hawthorne U Series

Lovestruck

Paradise Series

Devil's Angel

Wild Hearts

New York Billionaires Series

Billionaire Boss

Billionaire Grump

Billionaire Devil

Billionaire Romantic

Standalone Rom-com

Beautiful Savages

ABOUT THE AUTHOR

Julie Capulet is an Amazon top 20 bestselling author of contemporary romance. She writes steamy he-falls-first romance with heart, heat and fairy tale HEAs. Her stories are inspired by true love and she's married to her own real life hero. When she's not writing, she's reading, traveling, walking on the beach and watching rom-coms.

www.juliecapulet.com